I0747501

# THE PRINCE IS MISSING!

A KORI BRIGGS ADVENTURE

## A.P. RAWLS

UPPER WEST SIDE PRESS, LLC

The Prince is Missing!

*A Kori Briggs Adventure*

A.P. Rawls

FIRST PRINTING

ISBN: 978-1-7372613-9-1

eBook ISBN: 979-8-9869058-0-8

Large Print Edition: 979-8-9869058-1-5

Library of Congress Control Number: 2022916655

© 2022 A.P. Rawls

All Rights Reserved

No part of this book may be reproduced or transmitted in any form or by any means without the written permission of the publisher.

UWS

Upper West Side Press, LLC

This is a work of fiction. Names, characters, places, and incidents either are the product of the author's imagination, or are used fictitiously. Any resemblance to actual persons, living or dead, businesses, companies, events, or locales is entirely coincidental.

**The Kori Briggs series of adventure spy novels
by A.P. Rawls:**

### *The Dark Tetrad*

In this action-packed Kori Briggs debut novel, Kori is on the trail of a madman who has managed to steal a hundred pounds of uranium and, with the help of an equally twisted Russian scientist, is intent on detonating a nuclear bomb somewhere in the world. But when and where? Come along with Kori on this vicarious thrill ride as she follows clues from Washington, DC to New York City, Russia, Israel, and finally, Paris, the "City of Lights."

### *We'll Quit When We're Dead*

Everyone's favorite secret agent is once again globetrotting around the world to save the day. This time she's investigating a real and imminent threat from a foreign power, a potential terrorist act on American soil so extensive that its successful deployment could well result in World War III. Follow Kori from San Francisco to Vancouver to Istanbul as she races against time to prevent a cataclysmic collision with destiny.

*Danger Level 4*

In this third book of the A.P. Rawls series of Kori Briggs suspense spy thrillers, Kori has landed in the middle of a South American revolution. Super-secret spy organization Rampart has intelligence that a dictator with weapons of mass destruction is about to be overthrown. But who are the revolutionaries, and are they any less dangerous? The stability of the Western Hemisphere is at stake. Follow Kori through the jungles, hills, and perilous streets of a nation on the brink of war with itself!

*The Prince is Missing!*

In this fourth book of the series, Kori has been tasked with the assignment of finding England's missing Prince Grayson! All signs point to a kidnapping at the hands of an American ex-con, but Kori knows there's much more to the story. Follow her and her trusty Russian sidekick Anya Kovalev as they scour the grand city of London for clues to the prince's disappearance!

**Get a free gift when you register for updates at https://koribriggs.com/connect/**

**UWS**
**Upper West Side Press, LLC**

## A Note From the Author

As this book was going to print, Queen Elizabeth II passed away at the age of 96, having reigned as England's queen for seventy years. Through times of terrific change, Her Royal Majesty remained a paragon of loyalty and steadfastness. Her mention within this work of fiction is intended with the utmost respect and admiration.

—A.P.R.

Kingsley Moore carried the tray up the stairs, glancing down at it when he arrived at the anteroom door: tea, honey, yogurt parfait, banana nut bread, blackberry jam, linen napkin, two silver teaspoons, and one silver butter knife. It was all there, the same items Kingsley had delivered every morning for the past twenty years. And every morning, he'd come back later to retrieve the tray, sometimes empty, sometimes exactly as he'd delivered it.

Kingsley was born to be a valet. The vocation was in his blood. His father was personal valet to Prince Nicholas, Duke of Kent and his grandfather was personal valet to Prince Henry, Duke of Gloucester. It was the family business, a proud family, and it was no surprise, therefore, that Kingsley found himself also serving the royals, personal valet and chauffer to Prince Grayson, Earl of Kendal.

Of course, the job was not as prestigious as, say, personal valet to Charles, Prince of Wales and heir apparent to the British throne. Charles, after all, was internationally famous. Grayson, on the other hand, was the oft-forgotten fifth child of the queen, seventeenth in line for the throne once you factored in all the children and grandchildren of the earlier-born sons. The world would never see a King Grayson unless some monumental, cataclysmic event occurred—a meteor crashing into Buckingham Palace, for instance, with all sixteen heirs before him within.

Nevertheless, personal valet to a prince, seventeenth in line for the throne or seventeen-hundredth in line, was still a noble profession. In a world that had become coarse and vulgar, English royalty was an oasis of propriety, dignity, and decorum, not to mention grand historical tradition. This held true regardless of the level of fame, and the standard of decorum was upheld as much by the staff members as the royals themselves.

The pay was fair at best, a little-known secret of life with the royals, but Prince Grayson was otherwise generous, frequently handing Kingsley fifty-pound notes; always on a whim and at random times. The prince would be in a good mood. Kingsley might do nothing more than lay out the proper suit for the particular occasion of the day or properly arrange the prince's toiletries or assist him with a shave. A normal, everyday task, in other words. Nonetheless, the prince would slap fifty pounds in his hand and say, "Good man!" as if Kingsley had done the grandest of favors.

Prince Grayson wasn't always in a good mood. Kingsley suspected bipolar disorder, though as valet, the prince's mental state was not his concern. But, for the effective execution of his duties, it paid to have at least some understanding and so Kingsley had learned over the years, with no small success, how to read Grayson's emotional swings, sometimes anticipating them. Still, the highs and the lows often came out of the blue, defying any idea that there might be a predictable pattern.

By far, the best thing about being a valet for Prince Grayson, besides the noble calling of the profession itself, were the accommodations. The prince's residence, a Gothic-revival style manor in St. John's Wood, a thirty-minute drive to Buckingham Palace, was built in the Victorian era and boasted twelve thousand square feet of living area, including the servant's floor where Kingsley lived. And the servants' quarters were generous. Kingsley had more than a bedroom—it was more like a flat, complete with living room, large bath, even a small kitchen. The butler and maid, a married couple, lived on the premises as well in an equally large residence. There was a suite in the mansion for Grayson's private secretary, Parker Bates, but Bates preferred to live off-residence with his family in Brixton, arriving at the prince's manor every morning like clockwork at 8 a.m.

The prince, a single man of fifty-five, kept himself mostly to the third floor where the master suite was, a suite that made Kingsley's look like a cheap efficiency. Also on the third floor was the prince's study; a morning/breakfast room enclosed in glass and situated at the rear of the house that overlooked the stone courtyard below; a music room that the prince, being fairly non-musical, had converted into a media room complete with a large movie screen and state-of-the-art sound system; and a library, probably the least-used room in the house.

The second floor contained the servant's quarters and spare bedrooms. The first floor boasted an expansive foyer, kitchen, bar room, lengthy dining room, ballroom, billiard room, Parker Bates's office, and miscellaneous drawing rooms, each decorated in unique themes corresponding to a particular period. The official decorator of Buckingham Palace, sent to the manor by the queen herself, was responsible for the decorating. The prince had little interest in interior design and, in fact, used none of the rooms on the first floor. The manor was a showpiece of old English luxury, but Grayson rarely entertained guests. When he left his third-floor quarters, it was to leave the house, either for a royal event or obligation of some sort, of which there were too many for Grayson's comfort, or to visit his beloved club—White's, the legendary and exclusive London gentlemen's club in St. James, counting among its members only royalty, the super-wealthy, or the highly connected.

He was there on the preceding night, returning home around midnight, as Kingsley noted from his bedroom, having heard a taxicab pull up to the residence at that time. The prince was good like that. His nights at the club could run quite late, but rather than inconvenience Kingsley for a lift back to the manor, he was quite comfortable taking an ordinary taxicab. It was an ironic luxury that the older-born sons could never enjoy. The biggest advantage for Grayson of being fifth born and seventeenth in line for the throne was that he remained mostly out of the public's eye, which was perfectly fine with him. "The reclusive prince," as the media referred to him, when they referred to him at all, was rarely recognized in public and practically never in a dark taxicab in the middle of the night.

Kingsley, tray in hand, knocked quietly on the anteroom door, heard nothing, then proceeded through the anteroom, a room larger than his own bedroom, to the prince's bedroom door upon which he lightly rapped his knuckles.

"Sir?" he said softly.

With no response, he rapped louder. "Sir?" he spoke up. "Prince Grayson?"

Then he slowly pushed the door open, peering inside. He took a step forward and felt a strange draft in the room.

"Sir? I have your breakfast. It's nine o'clock, sir."

Across the large room, he could make out the master bed and realized it was unmade and empty. Then Kingsley noticed the open window at the back of the bedroom, its curtains waving lightly in the cool autumn breeze, the obvious source of the draft. The rest of the curtains of the room were drawn tight, keeping the room in a fairly dark state despite the time of day.

Kingsley felt a sense of alarm. Something wasn't right. He sat the tray down on a Louis XV fauteuil armchair, hesitated a moment, then flipped the light switch. With a sickening feeling he spotted a trail of blood running from the bed to the open window. He darted across the room, threw open the curtains, looked below, and saw nothing. In a panic, he raced about the master suite, checking the bathroom and the dressing room. Nothing was out of place. He left the master chamber and checked every room on the third floor, dashing in and out of the prince's study, the morning room, the media room, even the library.

"Sir?" he yelled out. "Prince Grayson!"

Then he ran back into the bedroom and looked again, dumbfounded, at the trail of blood and he knew that something terrible had occurred in that room the previous night.

Kingsley ran out of the chamber and flew down the steps, calling out for Grayson's personal secretary. "Bates!" he shouted. "Bates! The prince is missing! Prince Grayson is gone!"

**2**

—·—

"Mr. President, it is good to see you again." Rampart Director Richard Eaglethorpe, tall and trim, Black, with short, bristly gray hair, smiled and shook the hand of the president of the United States.

"Director Eaglethorpe," the president nodded. Then he turned to the woman standing beside the director, toned and athletic, with long, straight, dark hair. He smiled. "Agent Briggs. Always a sight for sore eyes."

"The pleasure is all mine, Mr. President," Rampart agent Kori Briggs smiled back, taking the president's hand.

"Well, please sit down," the president said, waving toward the chairs in front of his Oval Office desk. The three sat and the president, a sturdy man with a high forehead and dark, thinning hair, leaned forward. "Well, I'll get right to it because I'm sure you're wondering why I've invited you here, and so early in the morning to boot." Kori smiled to herself at the word choice. A call from the White House was never an invitation. A call from the White House was a summons.

"Whatever it is, Mr. President," said Eaglethorpe, "we remain at your disposal, of course." This was no mere politesse. Rampart was a super-secret American spy organization, but it was an autonomous one. Yes, the agents would answer a summons to the White House, but Rampart was not, in any official or formal way, at the disposal of the executive branch of the government, or of any branch, for that matter. The president was well aware of this; he'd seen to its independence himself. The country needed a protective agency not beholden to political agendas or whims, an agency that could focus on the task at hand without having to be concerned with outside interference. Rampart was that agency.

"Thank you, Richard," the president said. "I sleep better at night knowing I can depend on your team. Well, on to business then: an hour ago, I received a call from Prime Minister Oliver Harris. It seems the UK needs our help with a little something. Are you familiar with the case of Prince Grayson?"

"Yes, of course," nodded Eaglethorpe. Who wasn't familiar with it? The news had been filled with nothing else since Grayson's mysterious disappearance a week before. There were scant details. Buckingham Palace had released a curt statement that the prince was apparently missing, and this only after he had failed to turn up at a luncheon for a trade group and then a subsequent dinner engagement. Rumors began to fly and the paparazzi started camping out at the prince's mansion in St. John's Wood. The statement from the palace emphasized the idea that there was no immediate cause for alarm, yet failed to elaborate on why that was, serving only to further fuel the rumors.

"Well, it happens that they want our help in their investigation," said the president.

"Really?" said Eaglethorpe. "I would have assumed their National Crime Agency or even MI5 would be all over it. Why invite a foreign police agency? And why us?"

"Because, as it turns out, there is an American involved. The disappearance is more than just a disappearance. Two hours ago, PM Harris called after forwarding this to me." The president slid a sheet of paper across the desk, a printout of a typewritten letter:

*You're probably wondering where your prince is. Or if he's even still alive. Wonder no more. Rest assured the prince is alive and well, as you can see by the attached photo. Reasonably well, that is. But alas, I fear the time is running out for good Prince Grayson. His death is imminent. A mere week away. But of course, his life needn't end. There is a very simple solution. By separate correspondence, you will receive all the information you need to deliver to me the small sum (by your royal standards) of $100,000,000 (US). Once I have confirmed that the sum has been deposited properly, you will get your prince back. There. I cannot make it any more simple than that. Look to hear from me no more. By next Tuesday, you will have your prince and I will have my money; or you will have retained the money and your prince will be dead. The choice is yours.*

*Very sincerely yours,*
*Newton S. Dempsey*

"Wow," said Kori.

"'Wow' indeed," said the president.

"Sir, where was this sent?" Eaglethorpe asked.

"To Buckingham Palace. A special email account that only the prince could have known about—an account for royal matters only, monitored by the Lord Chamberlain of the Royal Household. It's about as high as it goes. For all intents and purposes, he might as well have sent it to the queen herself. Shortly after, an email came with instructions for the transfer of funds to an offshore account. It's virtually untraceable. The account is with a bank in the Channel Islands set up in the name of a trust formed in Liechtenstein and managed by nominees in Panama, none of whom appear to be real people. Of course, once the money is wired into the account, it will no doubt be funneled into a dozen other secret accounts around the world. Newton Dempsey, if you don't know the name, is a genius at this kind of stuff. Oh, here's the photo that's referenced." The president handed to Eaglethorpe a picture of Prince Grayson sitting on the edge of a bed in what appeared to be a rather luxurious hotel room. His scalp was bandaged, there was a bandage across his nose, and his eyes were blackened. Seated beside him was a thin, well-dressed, smiling man with a hawk nose and graying hair. He had his arm around Grayson as if they were best buddies. Grayson was not smiling.

"Well, sir, I do know the name, as a matter of fact. And that's him all right," said Eaglethorpe, looking at the picture. "Son of a bitch."

"Wait," Kori said, "I thought Dempsey was still locked up."

"Got out a year ago," said the president. "You remember the case, I take it?"

"We didn't work on it, but it was some kind of corporate fraud thing, wasn't it?"

"On a massive scale. Dempsey ran a bogus IT company. Falsified every financial document imaginable. Raised hundreds of millions of dollars for an essentially nonexistent organization."

"I remember reading the FBI file," said Eaglethorpe. "Gotta hand it to him. It was an amazing enterprise just in sheer audaciousness. He rented out high-end office space in Manhattan and filled it with a whole crew of actors. Then he invited investors from all over and put on an impressive show for them. Picked them up at the airport in a Rolls, wined them, dined them, put 'em up at the Four Seasons. He was advertising that he had 'the next great thing' and he'd bring the investors by the offices and have his actors do PowerPoint presentations that were so technical and convoluted that the poor saps he targeted had no choice but to believe every word. Then he loaded them up with impressive financials, all fake, of course, and told them that investment opportunities were limited and they'd better get onboard before the train left the station."

"FOMO," said Kori.

"Huh?" said the president.

"Fear of missing out, Mr. President. It's a powerful force."

"Indeed," nodded Eaglethorpe. "Dempsey was able to collect about one hundred million and then, of course, it all kind of went to hell when none of the investors started getting any of the returns they were promised. Found Dempsey in Costa Rica, as I recall. Living like a king."

"That's correct," said the president. "Served ten years of a thirty-year sentence. Released for good behavior, ironically."

"That's an interesting number he raised," Kori observed. "One hundred million. The same amount he's demanding now."

"Yes," said the president. "I noticed that. It's almost like he wants to replace the money he ultimately didn't get away with."

"Well, he hasn't lost any of his audaciousness," Kori remarked. "I mean, kidnapping a prince and holding him for ransom? And announcing right away that he's the kidnapper? Even sending a picture of himself? Talk about going all in. 'Audacious' doesn't even cut it."

"He thinks he can't get caught," mused Eaglethorpe. "He's arrogant. He thinks he's bulletproof. The photo is as much a taunt as it is evidence that he's got the prince."

"Well, he has his limits, apparently," said the president. "I mean, Prince Grayson? He could have grabbed Charles or Edward. Or even Anne. Or one of the kids . . . what're their names? Prince William or Harry? Grayson's the forgotten prince. When you think of British royalty, you never think of Grayson. He's like the Zeppo of the group."

"The what, sir?" Kori asked.

"See?" grinned the president, shooting a glance at Eaglethorpe who grinned in return.

"Never mind," the president chuckled. "The point is, the prime minister has it in his head that since the perpetrator is an American, the dirty work ought to fall to us. Or, at the least, we should assist."

"I would have thought that the NCA or MI5 would prefer to work on this themselves," said Eaglethorpe. "In secret. I'm sure they don't want this getting out. I mean, they've said nothing officially about a kidnapping."

"Truthfully, they need all the help they can get. They don't have a single lead on Dempsey's location. The prime minister feels we might be able to help. And I'll tell you, he sounded more than a little stressed."

"I'm sure."

"We can start investigating on our side of the pond, and determine if Dempsey is in contact with anyone here in the States. But you are right that they don't want any of this getting out. Frankly, it's a terrible embarrassment for them. How can you lose a prince to a glorified con man, no matter how audacious? Keeping the whole thing a secret is paramount. Indeed, that's why the prime minister called me. He's requesting the most top-secret people we have to assist MI5. Of course, that's you guys. If you're interested."

"Of course, Mr. President," said Eaglethorpe. "We're happy to jump right in, aren't we Agent Briggs?"

Kori had nothing in particular going on. Frankly, she'd been getting bored lately and Kori did not handle boredom well. "Very happy to help, sir," she said.

"We'll determine Dempsey's last known whereabouts before he headed for London," Eaglethorpe offered.

"Yes, uncover any information you can on him, Richard. Everything he's been up to since his release from prison and anyone he's been in contact with. And then I think we need to send your best agent to London to meet with MI5 and jump into the investigation over there. Ms. Briggs?"

Kori smiled. "It's been too long since I've been to London, Mr. President. I would welcome the opportunity."

"Excellent. Well, you two now know as much as I do about the case, so get going. And do keep me posted. The PM passed along to me the queen's sentiments. She's 'quite concerned,' he told me, which, from what I know of the queen, is about as emotional as she gets. Still, Grayson *is* her youngest son. A mother's love is a mother's love."

"Understood," Eaglethorpe nodded.

"That said," the president continued, "I should also report to you that she has no intention of paying the ransom. The prime minister wanted me to know that she was quite adamant on that point. We need to find the prince and bring him home alive."

"Of course, sir," said Eaglethorpe. "We understand entirely."

The president rose and the agents did likewise.

"Agent Briggs," said the president as he walked them to the door, "let's present the queen with a memorable, suitable gift, shall we? In addition to the return of the prince, of course."

"Sir?"

"Newton Dempsey. All wrapped up with a red, white, and blue bow."

"It would be my pleasure, sir."

# 3

Rampart headquarters were located on the top floor of a nondescript, glass office building on L Street. A secure, private elevator led to the small lobby of the agency with a sign outside the door that read, "Gladstone Conveyor. Simply the Best."

Having been briefed by Eaglethorpe as he and Kori were driving back to the office, Agent Darren Cooper tracked down the last known whereabouts of Newton Dempsey while agent James Foster prepared a brief on Dempsey's background.

"Looks like Bean Town," Cooper announced from behind a metal desk upon Eaglethorpe and Kori's arrival.

"Cool," Kori said. "Set me up, Coop."

Cooper, tapping away on his computer, said, "I'm making all the arrangements right now. And I'll get you some more specifics."

Meanwhile, agents Royce Gibson and Domenic Vasquez were searching multiple databases to access whatever information they could find on Prince Grayson's movements before the kidnapping.

Kori hung around, waiting on the intelligence file that the agents were collectively creating, grabbing a cup of coffee in the meantime and helping herself to the contents of the ever-present box of donuts. Then, with file and marching orders in hand, she drove home to her fourteenth-floor condo overlooking the Potomac. She changed into more comfortable clothing, packed lightly, then drove to Reagan National Airport for the ninety-minute flight to Boston Logan.

A short Uber ride from there, making use of the Ted Williams Tunnel, took her to her first stop.

"This is it, miss."

The driver pulled over in front of a narrow three-story row house. Kori looked at the peeling paint and the tattered awning above the front door and noticed that almost all of the houses on the street were more or less in the same condition. *This must be the only neighborhood in South Boston that hasn't been gentrified yet*, she thought.

She checked the note in her file to confirm the address, thanked the driver, and stepped out of the car. She looked up and down the street, then zipped up her black, Moncler hooded jacket against the brisk October air, and walked up the concrete steps to the door of the house. She knocked and a long face with a familiar hawk nose peered out from behind the door's window.

"Yes?"

"Russell Dempsey?" Of course, it was. He was a few years older than his brother Newton, but there was no mistaking the resemblance. As far as Cooper and Foster were able to determine from their digital sleuthing,

Newton Dempsey had been in contact with Russell more than anybody else since his prison release. No surprise there. They'd grown up in South Boston, back in the days when the streets were a little more rough and tumble. Their father had run out on them when they were kids and they'd been raised by their mother—a sometime waitress, sometime receptionist, sometime prostitute. Kori wondered how such a sophisticated swindler could come from such a humble background. But she knew that Russell and Newton had gone their separate ways; Russell stuck around the neighborhood and went to work at the local chemical plant, while Newton bounced around the country and became ever more adept at conning people out of their money. After his prison stint, he returned home and moved into an apartment three blocks from his brother, perhaps his last remaining friend.

"My name is Briggs. I'm an agent with the National Bureau of Criminal Investigations. May I come in for a moment?" Kori held up her photo ID, complete with a badge embossed with the logo of the faux organization, a cover she often used to question people. The name "Rampart" was never revealed to outsiders. And the "National Bureau" card always worked.

"Is this about Newton?"

"Yes, sir."

Kori heard the slide of a deadbolt lock and the door opened. "Okay, come in."

"Thank you." Kori stepped inside and glanced about the cramped living room. A worn sofa faced a small, flat-screen TV. Faded green walls held framed Red Sox posters and shelves of porcelain knick-knacks. A stack of old magazines shared a crowded coffee table with the television remote, an empty coffee mug, an ashtray, and an old Robert Ludlum paperback.

"Helen!" Russell Dempsey called out. "We have a guest."

Presently, a short, plump woman entered the living room from the kitchen, wiping her hands on her apron. "Oh, hello," Helen Dempsey smiled.

"Helen, this is . . . what did you say your name was?"

"Briggs," Kori said. "Agent Briggs with the National Bureau of Criminal Investigations."

"Oh, my," Helen said, furrowing her brow. "What has Newton done now?"

"Stop it, Helen," said Russell. "For crying out loud, we don't know that Newton has done anything. Please sit, Ms. Briggs." All three sat, Russell and Helen on the sofa and Kori in a folding chair adjacent to it. "Now what's this about? What can you tell me about Newton?"

"Well, the fact is, we are investigating your brother, Mr. Dempsey. But I'm not at liberty to say why."

"Do you know where he is?" Russell asked. "That's all I'm really interested in, Ms. Briggs. I haven't seen him for a month and I have to tell you that I'm just a little more than concerned."

"Of course, you are. Well, no, quite frankly, we don't know where he is. I'm aware that you filed a missing person report. Three weeks ago, to be exact."

"And haven't heard squat since. The police haven't done a damn thing. Worthless, if you ask me. So if my brother is missing, what kind of an investigation are you doing? You said you're with some bureau of criminal investigations? What's that?"

"We're an intelligence agency focused on high-level crimes."

"Well, I don't see the connection. Newton is as straight as an arrow. Yes, yes, Ms. Briggs, he did some bad things in the past, but he's paid his debt to society. Ten years, as a matter of fact. He's a new man now. Helen, why are you rolling your eyes?!"

"I wasn't rolling my eyes."

"You see, Ms. Briggs, my wife believes that once you're a criminal, you can never change. She didn't like Newton from the start."

"That's not true," Helen objected, crossing her arms and shaking her head.

"Oh, yes it is, and you know it."

"I liked him. I just never trusted him."

"Whatever. Ms. Briggs, what is my brother accused of exactly?"

"Again, Mr. Dempsey, I'm afraid I'm not at liberty to say. It's the nature of the investigation."

Dempsey frowned. "Well, if you're investigating a crime, you must have your reasons, right? And that means you must have some idea as to where my brother is. Or at least was. Now, what do you know about his whereabouts? I think I have a right to know. Certainly, there must be something you can tell me."

Kori had walked into the house without a strategy to get the information she wanted. She operated better on the fly, preferring to size up the situation first, assess the players, and respond accordingly. Now she knew what tack to take.

"Mr. Dempsey," she began, "without getting into too many details, I can tell you that we'd like to find your brother to clear him of any wrongdoing. That's why I'm here. You see, our white-collar crime division is looking into some recent corporate and banking irregularities in and around the greater Boston area. Your brother's name came to our attention from the NCIC database and—"

"The what?"

"The National Crime Information Center. All missing person reports get funneled through there. A quick cross-check of known white-collar criminals revealed your brother's name. Now, we have no reason to suspect he's guilty of anything. We imagine he's reformed, just as you've suggested. We'd just like to question him. Hopefully, to eliminate him as any kind of suspect."

Dempsey relaxed. "See, Helen? Newton hasn't done a thing. I told you."

"Mr. Dempsey," Kori just had to ask, "how can you be so sure that your brother hasn't committed any crimes since he's been out of prison?"

"Because Newton has completely changed," Dempsey replied. "I mean it. Hand to God, Ms. Briggs. Look, my brother was never a bad guy. You have to understand that when Newton and I were growing up, people from this neighborhood didn't have a lot of options. Most of us got jobs at one of the industrial plants around here. We worked hard and saved our money. We bought houses and lived our lives. But, as you can see, none of us are what you'd call wealthy.

"But Newton always wanted more. He felt that hard work was for suckers. So anyway, he fell in with some bad people after high school. He learned the tricks of the street. He sold drugs, he broke into some homes, passed a few bad checks, that sort of thing. Small stuff, you know? I tried to mentor him, tried to be the big brother. But Newton had plans. He always said he wanted to be rich. I mean *really* rich. 'I want to get out of this stinking place,' he'd always say. One day, he met a guy who got him involved in some fraudulent activities. Selling knockoff watches and stereo speakers and whatnot. I don't know . . . from there his interest in conning people out of their money just sort of grew. Exponentially, I would say. He learned everything he could. He started pulling all these scams, you see."

Kori let Russell talk even though he wasn't telling her anything she didn't already know. The FBI file on Newton Dempsey was pretty thick and represented a veritable laundry list of cons. The Jamaican switch, the Beijing tea scam, the bar bill scam, the Spanish prisoner, the melon drop—he learned them all. And the cons became more and more sophisticated. In time, he forayed into insurance fraud, stock fraud, foreign currency fraud, and real estate fraud. He learned enough about the business world that he could have earned an MBA from Harvard. Hell, he could have *taught* at Harvard. He pulled off elaborate Ponzi schemes and ran bogus investment companies.

Newton Dempsey got his wish. He got out of South Boston. Reportedly, he'd even managed to drop his working-class Southie accent. He traveled all around the country, never staying anywhere too long. Just long enough to pull off the latest fraud. Then he was off to a new location and a new mark or group of marks. He got rich, too, like he'd always wanted. But then it all came crashing down, as it always does, when he decided to pull off "just one more" scam. One to retire on. One to punch his ticket to the fraudster Hall of Fame. The fake New York City "Next Great Thing" scam had been a masterpiece. Some of the biggest names in New York fell victim to it. A couple of Hollywood celebrities, too. Even some international investors, and smart ones at that. The problem was, he'd had to involve too many people to make it work. Someone talked. Someone remembered him speaking of Costa Rica. The FBI took it from there.

"But all that's behind him, Ms. Briggs," Russell Dempsey was saying. "Ten years in prison changes a man. He came back home. He took a sales job at a car dealership. He got an apartment. He's completely settled down with no plans whatsoever to go back to his old life. He goes to church every Sunday, Ms. Briggs. Did you know that?"

As a matter of fact, she did. The FBI continued to surveil Dempsey. Russell was speaking the truth. The man's record since his release a year prior was spotless. He spent six months under supervised release and passed with flying colors. He was sincerely penitent about his crimes. It said so in the file. His priest had vouched for it. "Nelson is a changed man," he'd say to anyone who asked. "Proof that anybody can be redeemed by the forces of good in this world."

Maybe so. But then why was Dempsey in London demanding one hundred million dollars for the safe return of Prince Grayson, Earl of Kendal? Seemed as if the criminal mastermind couldn't stop committing crimes. Maybe he hadn't been redeemed after all.

"I have no reason to doubt you," Kori said to Russell, even though she had every reason to doubt him, "which is why we'd like to find him. Again, just to rule him out. I'm sure it won't be hard. Now, are you absolutely certain you have no idea where he could be?"

"Ms. Briggs, if I knew where he was, would I have filed a missing person report?"

"Yes, about that. Do you happen to remember the investigating officer's name?"

"Sure, I remember. Officer Joseph O'Rourke. He works out of the District C-6 station over on B Street."

"And I'm sure you probably went over everything with Officer O'Rourke, but if you could just humor me, I'd like to ask you some questions about your brother in the days before he went missing. Would that be okay?"

"Would it be okay? Ms. Briggs, it would be more than okay. O'Rourke spent a grand total of about three minutes with me. Barely asked anything. When Helen and I went to the station to file the report, we felt as if we were interrupting their day."

"I'm very sorry to hear that."

"Frankly, you're the first person to come along who's expressed any interest in my brother at all. So, please, by all means, fire away."

Kori asked a series of questions about Newton Dempsey but came away with nothing more than what a good guy he'd become. Russell spoke with pride about Newton's reclamation. He was certain that, above all else, Newton had left any bad influences behind. He was making it a point to surround himself only with good, honest, upstanding people. On the other hand, it didn't take an expert investigator to sense Helen Dempsey's cynicism. She continued to roll her eyes at her husband's praises. He glanced over at her impatiently from time to time, but eventually ignored her and kept his eyes focused on Kori as though nobody else were in the room.

Finally, Kori thanked them both for their time and rose to leave. "By the way," she said, "where exactly is the police station from here?"

"Six blocks down, three blocks over," Russell said. "You can't miss it. You'll probably find it a waste of time, but if you learn anything from those slackers, would you please let me know?"

"Of course, Mr. Dempsey. And thank you again."

Kori walked down the street toward the police station thinking over the conversation. In the course of her questioning, she'd asked repeatedly about friends or visitors of Newton in the days before his disappearance. Russell didn't know of any. All Russell knew was that he and Helen had expected Newton to come by for Sunday dinner three weeks ago but he never showed up. "I'd made a pot roast," Helen had chimed in. Newton didn't answer his phone, and when Russell accessed his apartment with his spare key, he was nowhere to be found.

The more Kori thought about the kidnapping, the more improbable it seemed. First, there was no evidence that Newton Dempsey had gone back to his old tricks. And it wasn't just Russell's approbation. The FBI reports, the priest's endorsement—everything seemed to confirm Dempsey's redemption. Well, everything except Helen Dempsey's eye rolls, but how much stock could Kori put in those? The fact was, Newton had a job, an apartment, and a new start in life. Why risk it?

More importantly, and more mysteriously, how does a guy, just a year removed from a ten-year prison term, put together and execute a plan to kidnap the prince of another country? Since his release, Newton hadn't even been out of the state of Massachusetts, let alone the country. For six months of supervised release, he wasn't even allowed to leave the US. Suddenly, he decides to take off for London to snatch a prince that most Americans didn't even know existed? For a million-dollar ransom? On the surface, it was preposterous.

In fact, had Kori not seen the photograph of Dempsey with his arm around Prince Grayson, she would have called Eaglethorpe to declare that they had the wrong suspect. But MI5 had confirmed the authenticity of the photo. Photograph forensic techniques, including ELA—error level analysis—allow investigators to find elements added to a photograph that are, in some way, inconsistent with the original. The picture of Dempsey and Grayson together was no photoshopped forgery. The career con man from Southie was sitting next to a prince from the English royal family.

And this is what was leading Kori to believe that Dempsey had an accomplice. How else could he have pulled it off? Okay, so Russell had no knowledge of any strange friends or visitors who Newton might have been in contact with, but that didn't mean there wasn't somebody out there. Did Russell follow him around 24/7? And no matter how improbable it seemed, the photo didn't lie. Dempsey, she concluded, wasn't quite as redeemed as everyone thought, which, of course, fit the profile of a serial fraudster.

Plus, Kori knew that the White House had contacted Homeland and established that Newton Dempsey had left the States two days after Russell had said he'd last seen him. Boston Logan International to London Heathrow. Oh, he committed the crime, all right. There was no denying it. But he didn't do it alone. Either way, though it had taken him a year, he was back in the game, looking for another big payoff. Helen was right to roll her eyes.

**4**

—·—

Officer Joseph O'Rourke was a gangly, tall drink of water with a long face and a short haircut.

"Sure, I remember something about him. Newton Dempsey, right?" O'Rourke stood behind the gray metal counter tapping on his computer. A corkboard hung on the wall behind him covered in wanted posters. "Yeah, here it is. Missing person. So, what did you want to know about him, miss?"

"Anything at all, really. Anything might be helpful."

"Are you a friend of the family or something?"

"I'm a private investigator hired by the family." There. That would do.

"Uh-huh. Well, listen, there's not much to tell. We checked the morgue, the local hospitals, and the jails. All the usual places. Then I dumped him into the NCIC database."

"Did you do any investigation?"

"Investigation?"

"Yes. Did you interview anybody? Check out his apartment? Talk to his neighbors? Coworkers?"

O'Rourke leaned forward, lowered his voice, and said, "Look, miss, this was an ex-con, okay? It's not like the pope went missing. Besides, he's a grown man in his fifties, not some ten-year-old kid who got snatched at the bus stop. We get these all the time. A week from now, he's going to show up telling everyone about the great time he had in Vegas or something. Maybe he's holed up in a hotel with a girl. Maybe he's on a drinking binge. Who knows? Like I said, he's in the NCIC database. If he turns up, he turns up."

"Stellar police work, officer."

O'Rourke's body tensed and he rose to his full height. "Is there anything else, miss?" he asked curtly.

"Oh, no, you've been just a world of help. Thanks a bunch."

Kori turned and strode out of the police station. With no help there, she had one more angle to try—search Dempsey's apartment. Fifteen minutes later, she arrived at the studio apartment on the third floor of a three-story rowhouse, picked the lock, and entered.

There was a sofa bed, an end table, and a small, flat-screen TV hanging on the wall. Otherwise, the walls were bare. The kitchen had a sink, a small stove, and a mini fridge. There was a bathroom, a single closet, and nothing more. Dempsey's home was barely bigger than your garden variety motel room. He'd been living frugally, that much was certain. Quite a descent from the sprawling mansion he'd owned in Costa Rica with the ocean view and private beach.

Kori glanced about for a computer and saw none. Then she rifled through the drawer of the end table, looking for what, exactly, she couldn't have said. Brochures of London? Maps? Research on the royal family? She came up with nothing. The closet had a few odds and ends on clothes hangers and a pair of worn shoes rested on the floor, but Kori presumed that Dempsey had taken most of his clothes with him. If his plan worked, he certainly wasn't ever going to return to this. *Nor would he return if his plan* didn't *work*, Kori thought. However it turned out, Russell Dempsey had most likely seen the last of his brother.

Finally, Kori dumped the contents of the kitchen garbage can onto the floor. Coffee grounds, an empty cereal box, three empty Sam Adams beer bottles, a black banana peel, and a slip of paper that was, upon closer inspection, a receipt. Kori held it up to the light coming in through the tiny kitchen window. "O'Shaughnessy's Irish Pub." Two entrées: fish and chips and shepherd's pie. Four Guinness drafts. The receipt was dated the day before Dempsey's flight to Heathrow. *Interesting.*

Kori looked at her phone map and saw that O'Shaughnessy's was only four blocks away. She looked at the time and saw that it was a bit early for dinner, but so what? A Guinness and an order of fish and chips sounded pretty good. And she'd certainly make it a point to tip better than Dempsey had.

Kori sat at the long wooden bar sipping her Guinness and listening to the Irish folk music piped softly over the pub's speakers, the song "Black Velvet Band" at that particular moment. She glanced about the pub. It was a weekday and not yet dinner hour, but there were more than a few people scattered around at tables.

A trio of older men were sitting at the other end of the bar and one of them was just getting to the punchline of a joke: "So the first guy said, 'Those aren't oars, those are me sisters!'" This had the trio rolling with laughter and Kori found herself trying to imagine what the first part of the joke was.

"Your fish and chips will be out shortly, ma'am," said the bartender, a strapping twenty-something man with dark hair and a five o'clock shadow.

"Thanks," said Kori. "Hey, can I ask you a question?"

"Sure."

"You work here often?"

"Every day pretty much. Why?"

Kori pulled out her phone and showed the bartender a picture of Newton Dempsey. "You recognize this man?"

"Yeah, he comes in here from time to time," the bartender replied. "Can't say I've seen him lately, though."

"Do you remember the last time you saw him?"

"Hmm . . . not really."

"Think hard. It's important."

"Why? Is he missing or something?"

"Yep. He's missing and I'm investigating on behalf of the family."

The bartender scratched his head. "Well, let's see. Had to have been a few weeks ago, I suppose. He was in here with another guy, as I recall."

"Oh?" That explained the receipt with two dinner entrées.

"Yeah, nobody I'd ever seen before, though. I'm pretty good with faces and I'm sure I hadn't seen his before. They sat at that table right behind you."

"You have a good memory."

"Well, it seemed odd to me because your man always came in alone. That was the first and only time I ever saw him with anyone. Anyway, they ordered at the bar and then went over there and sat down."

"Do you remember anything about the other guy?"

"Not really."

"Do you remember maybe how old he was?"

"Hmm . . . probably younger than your man, if I had to guess."

"Tall? Short?"

"Tallish, I think."

"Heavy? Thin?"

"Truthfully, I don't remember him being either way. Average, I guess." The bartender shrugged. "Sorry I can't be more help."

"No, that's fine, thanks. I appreciate it."

"Oh, there is one thing. Neither talked very much, but the other guy had an accent."

"An accent?"

"Yep. British accent, I believe."

"Really? Thanks."

"Sure. Well, I hope you find him. I'm sure the family is worried. I'll go check on your fish and chips."

And there it was. The accomplice. If she could find him, she could find Dempsey. And if she could find Dempsey, she could find Prince Grayson. But all she knew was that the accomplice was no doubt in England now. A man in England with a British accent. Tallish. Neither heavy nor thin. That would limit the search to what, fifteen million people?

Of course, there was one thing Kori could do to try to narrow the field. She pulled out her phone, called Director Eaglethorpe, and explained her discovery.

"So listen, Chief, why don't we get the flight manifest from Homeland for the flight Dempsey took to London and start checking on the names of all the male passengers from the UK within, say, fifteen years of Dempsey's age? I'm sure they traveled together. In fact, the mystery man probably had the seat next to Dempsey's. That would be the place to start, no?"

"Good idea, Agent Briggs," said Eaglethorpe. "I'll get Foster working on it forthwith. We'll compile a list, run some background checks, and see what turns up."

"Sounds good. But, listen, I have to tell you, Chief, something is awfully strange about this case."

"Yeah? How so?"

"This guy, Dempsey. I mean, obviously, he's involved. Still, it seems like an odd venture for him. Kidnapping?

Based on what I've uncovered, he doesn't really fit the profile."

"Well, Briggs, first of all, I'm not sure there even *is* a profile. How many case studies can you think of that include the kidnapping for ransom of a prince?"

"Hmm . . . none offhand . . ."

"And look at this guy's past, for crying out loud. He's not a choir boy."

"Yes, but that's just it. His past. He hasn't committed a crime in ten years."

Eaglethorpe chuckled. "Kori, maybe that's because, oh, I don't know, he's been in prison?"

"I know, I know. What I mean is that he really seems to have gone straight. You should have heard his brother talk about him. He's ready to canonize him. And even the FBI says he's been clean as a whistle. He goes to church every Sunday."

"So did Lizzie Borden."

"She was never convicted, you know."

"You know, Kori, Freud believed that our personalities are set in stone by the age of five."

"Yeah, well Freud also believed that all men want to have sex with their mothers and murder their fathers."

"My point, Briggs, is that guys like Dempsey don't change."

"Okay, Chief, let's assume for the moment that that's true. But why start with something like this? He's been out of the game for a decade, right? So don't you think he'd start a little smaller? Get warmed up? Maybe hustle someone in a pool hall? Write a bad check? Secure a credit card under a fake name? He hasn't done any of those things, so far as we know. Flying to England to kidnap a royal is a pretty big leap, even for a guy with Dempsey's past, and even assuming he's still in the crime business."

"Maybe. But on the other hand, he's had ten years to plan something like this, Kori. He's shown himself to be pretty creative. And brazen. You give Dempsey ten years to scheme something, and I'll bet that scheme is going to be pretty monumental."

"I guess so. Still, it doesn't sit right with me."

"And, as you know, I respect your instincts, Agent Briggs. We'll get to the bottom of this. We always do. Toward that end, Cooper's got you on the first flight for Heathrow in the morning. An agent from MI5 will pick you up at the airport. I'll forward you the contact information. Hopefully, by the time you land, Foster will have some information on Dempsey's fellow passengers."

"Okay, sounds good. I'll check in from London."

"Please do. And don't forget the timetable, Agent Briggs. We're down to six days before the deadline Dempsey has given. And remember, the queen's not planning to pay."

"Brrr. That seems a little cold, doesn't it?"

"It's their policy, from what I understand. They never negotiate. But who knows? Maybe she's bluffing. Let's not put it to the test, okay? Let's find the prince."

"Right, Chief."

Kori ate her fish and chips, downed another Guinness, then took an Uber to the Parker House, her hotel for the night. Built in 1855 and rebuilt in 1927, the Parker

House was the longest continuously operating hotel in the United States. Guests included most every president since Ulysses S. Grant. Mark Twain stayed at the hotel, as did Charles Dickens. Perhaps more important than anything, the Parker House was the birthplace of the Boston cream pie.

From her suite, Kori called her mother to check in and to tell her yet another fictitious story about where she was and why. Rampart agents were sworn to secrecy; they couldn't even confide in their closest family members about their true occupations. Joan Briggs believed her daughter was the regional vice president of Gladstone Conveyor, with their headquarters not far from Joan's home in Alexandria where Joan lived with Baxter, her Jack Russell terrier. Kori told Joan a partial truth this time. She was in Boston. But then she said she'd be there for a week overseeing a huge installation at a new distribution center. "It's really involved," she told her. "It's completely automated and tied in with their computer system. But I'll call you when I get home. We'll have dinner, okay?" There. That gave her a weeklong excuse for being away.

It was still relatively early when Kori hung up. The sun had set and the autumn air of New England had gotten chillier, but she decided to go for a walk anyway. Kori could never sit still for long. The Parker House was only a couple blocks from the Boston Common, the city's famous public park, and she enjoyed a stroll around the grounds, ultimately taking a seat on a bench along Frog Pond watching the people go by and then deciding that it was time for a warm nightcap back at the hotel bar. An

Irish coffee would hit the spot. And it wouldn't be the worst thing in the world in Rampart agent Kori Briggs's mind if that coffee was served with a slice of the Parker House specialty—that Boston cream pie of theirs.

**5**

— · —

By the time Kori's plane touched down at London Heathrow airport, Agent James Foster, back in Rampart's DC office, had texted her a list of male passengers from Dempsey's flight manifest. Dempsey had taken a seat in coach next to a window. Beside him had been a five-year-old girl; the aisle seat had been occupied by the girl's mother. No help there. Foster and Agent Darren Cooper had narrowed the list of other passengers to eighty-five men, forty of them within ten years of Dempsey's age, and twenty-three of that subset from the UK. Out of those twenty-three, only one had a criminal record. Spenser Burke from Camden Town had done time in London's Belmarsh Prison for embezzling from a warehousing and shipping company of which he'd been the controller. He'd also been convicted of a few petty crimes in his youth—fighting, disorderly conduct, shoplifting. Surely, Spenser Burke was a place to start.

Exiting the airport into the cool London air, Kori noticed a man holding a sign that read: *Ms. Estella Havisham.*

"Hello, I'm Miss Havisham," Kori smiled, approaching the man.

"Pleased to meet you, Miss Havisham, I'm sure," said the man, tall, broad-shouldered with black, wavy hair and smoky, gray eyes. "I'm Samuel Pickwick. I have a car waiting if you'll kindly follow me."

Inside the car, the MI5 agent revealed his real name. "Victor Graham, at your service, Agent Briggs. I'm heading the investigative task force."

"Pleased to meet you, Victor. I had no idea you guys at MI5 were so well-read."

Graham chuckled. "Just our little joke, Agent Briggs."

"Kori, please."

"Kori. Glad you picked up on it."

"Of course. Estella Havisham from *Great Expectations* and Samuel Pickwick from *The Pickwick Papers*. Dickens characters. How wonderfully appropriate."

"Well, we could all use a little levity these days," Graham said as he drove east out of Heathrow toward London. The flight had been six hours and the time difference was five hours. It was now early evening in England and already dark. "So you're with the CIA, I presume."

"I'm with an American intelligence agency," Kori replied. "And that's about all I can say, I'm afraid."

"Oh, I see. A secret agency, eh? You know, I've heard rumors of a super-secret American intelligence agency."

"Really? Well, I wouldn't trust those rumors, Victor. You know how rumors can be. So, where are we headed?"

"I thought I'd take you to your hotel. The Savoy, right? That's what they told me. I must say, whatever agency you're with, your expense accounts are pretty generous."

"We prefer to travel in style."

"Yes, quite. At any rate, I thought we'd talk along the way. It's about an hour's drive. So, what can you tell me about your man Dempsey? We're quite keen on learning what you know."

"Well, of course, I'm happy to fill you in, Victor, and I appreciate the lift to the hotel, but I've already lost most of the day. Time change and long flight and all that. I'd like to go straight to the scene of the crime if I could."

"The scene of the crime? You mean the prince's manor house?"

"Of course. That's where I'd like to start. I can check into the hotel later."

"I see," Graham said, his brow furrowing. "Well, with all due respect, Kori, we've gleaned all we could from there, I'm afraid. Your help there isn't really what we need. As far as the investigation goes, we're quite capable of handling things on our end. We're MI5, you know, and we've been at this intelligence and security game quite a while. I have to tell you that we've quite completed our investigation of the crime scene."

The conversation was heading in a direction Kori didn't expect. "But then I'm a bit confused, Victor. Why did you enlist our help?"

"Truthfully, we just need to know what you've got on Dempsey, really."

"That's all? What we have on Dempsey?"

"Yes, frankly."

"We could have done that with a phone call."

"Yes, I said as much to our chief. But for some reason, he insisted on your presence. I believe he has orders directly from the prime minister. I think it's an overreaction. To be perfectly honest with you, the PM is in a bit of a panic over this kidnapping business. It doesn't look good, as I'm sure you can imagine. The press is having a field day with it. And so he's enlisted the help of you Yanks. Frankly, it's quite unnecessary, if you ask me. Oh, no offense, of course, Kori."

"None taken," Kori said, her jaw tightening. So that's how it was going to be. She had orders—from the president, no less—to help with an investigation where no help was being asked for. She had information on the kidnapper and that was all MI5 needed her for. But Kori didn't answer to MI5. She answered to Rampart director Richard Eaglethorpe who had promised the president that Rampart would take an active role in solving the case and rescuing the prince. Not only that, she'd made a personal pledge to the president: to present the queen with Newton Dempsey all wrapped up with a red, white, and blue bow.

"Well, here's the thing, Victor," Kori said, "I've been tasked with finding Dempsey. My orders come from the president of the United States. Now, my interest is not in stepping on anyone's toes or interfering in any way. I'm sure your investigation thus far has been top-shelf. MI5's reputation is sterling. And when this whole thing is over, I'd be thrilled to have you guys take all the glory. We don't need it. Our agency's practice is to avoid it, in fact. But whether you feel as though you need us or not, we're going to investigate this crime. That's what I've been sent here for, and that's what I'm going to do. We'll start with the manor house and then go from there."

"I see, Agent Briggs."

*Hmm...What happened to "Kori"?* Suddenly, it seemed as if the playful Dickens thing was a very long time ago. Damn shame. Those smoky, gray eyes hadn't left her mind.

"And what makes you think we will cooperate to the degree you're asking?" Graham continued. "As I said, the grounds of the prince's manor have been thoroughly investigated. There simply is no reason for me to take you there."

"Well, I can think of one reason, Agent Graham."

"Which is?"

"You'll take me there if you wish to learn what I know about Newton Dempsey."

"I see," said Graham. Then he was quiet, apparently mulling things over in his head. "Well, you seem determined, Agent Briggs," he said at last.

"Indeed I am, Agent Graham."

Graham sighed. "Then I suppose we will pop over to the prince's house."

"Thank you, Agent Graham."

"You're quite welcome, I'm sure, Agent Briggs."

On the way, Kori shared with Graham the name "Spenser Burke" from Camden Town, telling him how she'd uncovered the fact that Dempsey was not working alone. "We don't know anything for sure," she told him, "but it's a lead certainly worth following up on." Graham managed a nod of appreciation and called the name into MI5 headquarters. The hunt for Burke was on.

At Prince Grayson's manor house in St. John's Wood, Graham and Kori brushed past a few members of the paparazzi who'd been hanging out in front of the house. "Any news on the prince?" one of them yelled out as the pair accessed the steps leading to the entry. One of a few bobbies on duty nodded to Graham at the front door and unlocked it for him. Graham and Kori entered the house and the bobby quickly closed the door behind them.

"You see?" said Graham. "Every time we come back here, we're met with those media vultures out front."

"What have you been telling them?"

"Only that the prince is missing. But our continued presence here suggests foul play and that stokes the rumor mill. You can't believe the bollocks that some of these rags publish. Come along, Agent Briggs." Graham led the way through the foyer and up the main staircase. "The master suite is on the third floor."

The suite had been left untouched since the kidnapping. Kori noticed the unmade bed and the trail of blood that led from it to the window, about twenty feet away.

"Of course, we identified the blood," Graham said. "As expected, it's the prince's. The more or less straight line of the blood to the window, without a lot of extraneous spatters, means he was most likely accosted in his bed and then dragged directly to the window, probably unconscious. We assume he was hit with a blunt instrument on the forehead that produced a gash that ran down his face. That would be consistent with the photograph, too, as I'm sure you've seen. His nose was probably broken as well; the photo shows a bandage across his nose and two black eyes. We believe the prince might have fought back from his bed before being knocked out, thus the broken nose."

"He was awakened by the intruder's entrance."

"So it would seem."

"He didn't scream out?"

"If he did, nobody in the household heard him. Maybe the intruder put a hand over his mouth. So, after a short struggle in the bed, the prince was knocked out, and then carried to the window. Now, you'll notice the blood pooled at the base of the window."

"He was held there for a short time," Kori surmised.

"It appears so. We suspect that Dempsey was trying to figure out just how to get him out of the window and down to the ground."

"It wasn't Dempsey who held him," Kori said.

Graham nodded. "Yes, we came to the same conclusion. The prince is not a particularly big man, but, nonetheless, it would take some doing to physically manhandle him through the bedroom, out of the window, and, presumably, down a ladder to the ground. Dempsey's in his fifties and not exactly in tip-top shape. Perhaps this Burke fellow did the dirty work. Or perhaps it was both."

"Seems strange that Dempsey and/or Burke would come here without a solid plan as to how to remove the prince. Dempsey's a master planner."

"Yes, but then from what we understand, this is the man's first kidnapping, isn't it?"

"What about security cameras?"

"None."

"Alarm system?"

"Not functioning at the time."

"Seriously? Good God, this is the home of a prince."

"Yes, quite. From what we have ascertained, security was extraordinarily lax here. The prince often comes in late at night. He had a history of accidentally tripping the alarm and it appears as though it was deactivated on the night in question, presumably to avoid his tripping it when he returned. And apparently, the prince never liked the idea of cameras. Too intrusive, he said."

"I'll bet he's regretting that now."

"No doubt."

"What about the forensics report? Can I get a copy?"

"I suppose that can be arranged. There is scant DNA evidence and zero fingerprints. Certainly, the culprits wore gloves. The instrument that was used to hit the prince was apparently taken with them. From what we can gather, nothing of the kidnappers was left behind."

"You've had rain lately. I presume the ground is soft. Did you find evidence of a ladder?"

"Um, yes, indeed we did. Quite right. There were imprints in the ground below the window, as one would naturally expect."

"No wonder they knocked him unconscious."

"Indeed. Who wants to try climbing down a ladder while clutching a struggling kidnap victim? It's hard enough with dead weight."

"Not necessarily," said Kori. "I have a cousin who's a firefighter. You lay the unconscious person across your arms while you hold tight to the ladder and you carefully lower yourself one rung at a time. Meanwhile, you have a second person behind you, supporting you with his hand on your back end."

"Yes, evidently, that's the way it unfolded."

"And they took the ladder with them? Along with the prince?"

"Evidently."

Kori was thoughtful for a moment. "I don't know. This whole operation of Dempsey's seems half-assed, if you'll pardon my Americanism. I mean, why didn't they just take the prince out of here at gunpoint?"

"Well, first of all, Ms. Briggs, guns aren't quite as easy to come by over here as they are in America. Handguns are illegal. Now, I suppose Dempsey's accomplice might have been able to access one. He could have had a sporting rifle or shotgun, which are legal with a license, or he could have bought whatever he needed on the black market. But the fact is, for whatever reason, their preferred strategy seemed to be to just bop our prince on the head and take him away in an unconscious state."

"And lug him down a ladder from a third floor."

"So it would seem."

Kori noticed an open doorway on the far side of the bedroom and followed it into a spacious dressing room. Along the wall stood shelves of shoes and racks of clothes. Pricey stuff, too, Kori observed. Desmond Merrion suits and Salvatore Ferragamo shoes and Versace shirts and pants. She spied a Brunello Cucinelli sweatsuit and a Landon lambskin bomber jacket.

"The prince has expensive taste in clothes," she said.

"Yes, I must say he's quite the dresser," Graham said. "Everything custom tailored, no doubt. Now, is there anything else, Agent Briggs, that you need to see here in the bedroom? I do believe I have held up our end of the bargain, wouldn't you agree?"

Kori didn't need to see anything else. It had never been her belief that she would somehow magically uncover some piece of evidence that MI5 had missed. But she'd needed to see the scene. It was important on an instinctual level to get a feel for not only what happened, but where and how it had happened. She'd needed a picture in her mind. Now she had it.

"No, Agent Graham, I don't need to see anything else. You've been very patient. I would like to talk with the valet, however. He's the one who discovered the prince was missing, correct? The next morning?"

"Yes, Kingsley Moore. He's staying with relatives. We've had everyone clear out of the house until the prince is found. We consider the entire manor a crime scene. But, again, Agent Briggs, I don't see the point. We've interviewed Mr. Moore quite extensively, I assure you. Also the butler, the maid, and Prince Grayson's private secretary. Those were the people in the house that morning. Unfortunately, none were able to shed any light on what went on here during the night. Now, if you'd like, I can get you transcripts of those interviews. Will that suffice, Agent Briggs?"

It would not suffice, but Kori made a determination then and there that collaborating with Agent Victor Graham and MI5, notwithstanding Agent Graham's smoky, gray eyes, was going to be a dead end. Clearly, she was going to have to drag whatever information she needed out of MI5; none would be given easily. Just as well. Kori preferred investigating on her own anyway. Investigation by committee—indeed anything by committee—always tested Kori's patience.

"Yes, that will suffice," she replied.

"Very well. We'll swing by HQ and I'll give you copies of those transcripts. While we're there, you can tell us what you know about Dempsey. I believe that was the deal we struck, yes, Agent Briggs?"

# 6

The Savoy Hotel, sitting on the Strand in Central London, opened its doors in 1889. Impresario Richard D'Oyly Carte built it with the proceeds from his wildly popular Gilbert and Sullivan opera productions. It was the first true luxury hotel in London, indeed, in all of the United Kingdom. Private bathrooms, hot running water, elevators, and the new miracle of human innovation—electric lighting—made the hotel a destination all its own for the rich and famous of the time.

The rich and famous still stay at the Savoy. Over the years, guests have included Claude Monet, Oscar Wilde, Enrico Caruso, Harry Truman, Audrey Hepburn, Babe Ruth, Judy Garland, Marlon Brando, Bob Dylan, Marilyn Monroe, John Wayne, Louis Armstrong, the Beatles, Elton John, Elizabeth Taylor, Frank Sinatra, U2, and pretty much anybody else who's famous and sets foot in London.

On this night, one of the hotel's not-so-famous guests, by design, was Rampart secret agent Kori Briggs. She had told Graham what she knew about Dempsey at

Thames House, headquarters for Military Intelligence, Section 5, otherwise known as the Security Service, but most commonly referred to simply as MI5. The agency was created for domestic counterintelligence and security, often working hand-in-hand with MI6, which is more international in its scope. The investigation of the prince's kidnapping had started with the National Crime Agency, the British equivalent of the FBI, but due to its seriousness, had been kicked up to MI5, with Victor Graham appointed as head of the investigation.

By the time Kori and Graham had arrived at Thames House, it had been determined that Spenser Burke of Camden Town was missing from his residence. Kori had listened as Graham was briefed by another agent. Burke had been out of Belmarsh for about three years. He'd bounced around from job to job, doing mostly menial labor. Turns out, nobody wanted to hire an accountant who'd been put away for embezzlement. Yes, he'd flown to America and then come back, at least according to flight records, but nobody in his small circle of friends or neighbors had seen him since he'd left for Boston a few weeks before. Burke was in his late thirties, six foot, three inches, 200 pounds, and reportedly fit. A good candidate for knocking a man unconscious and then carrying him down a ladder. And the description, Kori noted to herself, wasn't far off from the one given by the bartender at O'Shaughnessy's. If Burke wasn't the accomplice, he'd do until the real one came along.

In a conference room with Graham and several other MI5 agents assigned to the case—all of them with arms folded and cool expressions—Kori revealed what she'd learned about Dempsey, including the conversation she'd had with his brother in South Boston. She talked a little about his previous criminal background, but the group already seemed to be up to speed on Dempsey's past. Graham thanked Kori for the information and then called a cab for her.

And that was that. Her presence was no longer required. They had everything they needed. Kori phoned Eaglethorpe from her hotel room and briefed him on the situation.

"Well, that's unfortunate," Eaglethorpe said. "So basically, you're on your own?"

"It would seem so. Those guys treated me like the proverbial turd in the punch bowl."

"Listen, why don't I call the president? He'll call the prime minister and we'll get you back in there."

"I don't think so, Chief. All that would do is sow more resentment. These guys seem to be taking it personally that the PM brought in help. I don't know, I guess I can't blame them. How would we feel if, in the middle of one of our investigations, the president sent an MI6 guy into our midst?"

"I guess we'd resent it."

"Of course. No, I think we're better off if I just go about investigating on my own. Besides, sometimes it's better to come at these things clean, with no outside influences, you know?"

"Agreed. But there's not much to be gained by you having to take the time to discover what's already known."

"True, but Graham was at least good enough to provide me with a pretty hefty file of what they've done so far, including transcripts of interviews."

"No doubt to cover his butt, Kori. If the PM asks, Graham wants to be able to say he's working with us, freely sharing information."

"Most likely. But let me see what I can do with it."

"Fair enough, but if you run into too many dead ends, I'm calling the president and getting you back in there."

"Understood. Meanwhile, I'll do my homework here tonight and get up to speed with the file. First thing tomorrow, I'll begin my investigation. I think I'll start by questioning the valet. Graham says he's with relatives, but that's all he'd say."

"No address in the file?"

"Nope. And apparently, all the interviews of the staff took place at MI5 headquarters."

"What's the valet's name?"

"Kingsley Moore."

"Wow, how British can you get?"

"Right?"

"Okay, I'll have Cooper do a complete search on him. We'll get you a probable location by morning."

"Thanks."

"You'll still have a lot of work ahead of you and not much time. Want some help? I could send Kovalev."

Kori brightened. "Chief, Would you? Her presence would really be appreciated."

"Sure, Briggs. I'll call her now. Hmm . . . it's probably around one in the morning in Moscow."

"She won't mind, Chief. Tell her it was my idea and that I'll buy her a vodka when she gets here. Maybe even two."

Kori spent the night in her room poring over the file from MI5. She read the witness interviews and studied the crime scene report. A timeline of events and floor plan of the manor were included. Strangely, there was no note of the imprints of a ladder below the window that Graham had mentioned. An oversight? Or was it possible that Graham wasn't sharing the full report? It was a small point, but it made Kori wonder what other details might be missing.

Eventually, she turned on the TV and caught a recap of the day's news. An MI5 spokesperson had held a press conference but had nothing new to share about the investigation into the prince's disappearance. He spoke vaguely and stuck to prepared remarks, taking only a few questions before bringing the presser to a close. There had been a statement from Buckingham Palace: The queen was "optimistic" that her youngest son would be found alive and well very soon and she commended the "astute and steadfast work" of all the agencies involved with the prince's "imminent and certain return."

Finally, bleary-eyed and in need of sleep, Kori closed the file, undressed, and slipped into bed. She rose as the sun was coming up. It looked like it was going to be a beautiful autumn day in London. A text from Cooper indicated a most-likely address for Kingsley Moore, and a text from Eaglethorpe told her that Russian-based Rampart agent Anya Kovalev would be arriving at Heathrow early that afternoon.

Kori showered, dressed, looked over the file once more, and then answered the knock at the door—room service delivering "The Savoy Breakfast" she'd ordered: coffee, tea, five different kinds of bread, croissants, Danish pastries, eggs, bacon, sausages, and Stornoway black pudding. *Cripes, how many people do they think are staying here?* she thought as she tipped the room service waiter. Even so, she ended up making a considerable dent in the offering, figuring she was in for a long day and deciding that she needed her strength.

Cooper's research revealed that Kingsley Moore had a sister in Hackney, a thirty-minute cab ride from the Savoy. There was very little other family anywhere in the London area, and Rosalie's was the obvious place Kingsley would have gone. Rosalie Shaw was older than Moore by a few years and married. She and Kingsley were close, Cooper's report said, though Rosalie hadn't followed their father into the domestic service industry. She was a private piano teacher and her husband, Jacob, was a marketing manager. They were a childless couple who frequented the theater and enjoyed small get-togethers with friends. Rosalie and Jacob seemed to do okay for themselves, Kori observed when the cabbie dropped her off in front of the Shaw's tidy Georgian-style, red brick rowhouse on a street facing a park.

From outside, Kori could hear someone banging away on a piano within, plodding their way through scales and not doing a very good job of it. A beginner student of Rosalie's, no doubt. Kori rang the bell and was surprised that Kingsley Moore himself answered, most likely an occupational habit. *Nice work, Coop,* she thought.

"Mr. Moore?"

"Yes, but I really have nothing more to say, I'm afraid," Kingsley said. "There's nothing newsworthy I can add. I've been telling all the media outlets the same thing and we would please ask that you respect our privacy." He started to close the door.

"Oh, but I'm not with the media," Kori said, wedging a foot into the door.

"You're not?"

"No, sir."

"Then who are you?"

"I'm an agent with an American intelligence service, sent here on behalf of the president of the United States to investigate the prince's disappearance."

Kingsley looked Kori over, trying to determine whether she was putting him on.

"It's true," Kori said, pulling out her National Bureau of International Criminal Investigations ID.

Kingsley swiped it from her hand and looked it over. "So why is the US investigating the kidnapping of a British prince, madam?" he asked.

"How much do you know about the investigation, Mr. Moore?"

"I daresay, very little."

"Well, you were there. You know it was a kidnapping. I don't think I'm betraying any significant confidence in telling you that the presumed kidnapper has been identified as an American. Consequently, we were contacted. By your prime minister, no less."

"I see."

Kingsley was still skeptical, and for the time being, Kori's foot was the only thing keeping the door open. Meanwhile, inside the house, piano keys continued to be pounded away on.

"Mr. Moore, if you're so inclined, might I suggest you call Agent Victor Graham of MI5? He's the lead investigating officer and will be able to vouch for my role here." It was a gamble. Graham might very well tell Moore not to talk to her. But Kori knew that Graham had interviewed Kingsley Moore and Moore would have recognized the name. Dropping it, along with the suggestion to call him, gave her credibility. Enough, hopefully, to open the door. She doubled down. "I'll wait out here while you call. Tell Agent Graham that Agent Kori Briggs is at your door." She removed her foot from the door and took a step backward.

Kingsley was quiet for a moment and then relaxed his cautious expression. "Very well, Ms. Briggs. Do come in."

Kingsley bowed slightly and waved Kori into the front drawing room of the house in a regal manner that she imagined he had done a million times. "Please have a seat.

I'll be with you in a moment." He retreated to a side room from where the offending piano sounds had been coming. Kori looked around the neat, smartly decorated drawing room, her eyes resting on a set of bookshelves loaded with classic English literature. *Music* and *literature,* she thought. *A very well-bred English family.* Presently, the piano banging stopped and a young girl about ten years old in a tweed skirt came out with a handful of sheet music, followed by a matronly woman with a curly, gray perm.

"Beg your pardon, miss," the woman said. "I didn't realize we had company."

"Oh, it's quite all right," Kori smiled. "Please don't stop on my account." Turning to the girl, she added, "You sounded just divine." Might as well earn some courtesy points, she figured. Couldn't hurt.

The girl smiled shyly and the woman, Rosalie, Kori presumed, said, "Oh, it's no problem. We were just about finished anyway, weren't we, Maggie?" Maggie nodded. "Okay, then," Rosalie continued, opening the front door, "off you go. Keep practicing those scales, young lady. Practice, practice, practice."

"Yes, ma'am, I will," Maggie said and then she was out the door.

"Well," Rosalie said, turning back to Kori, "My brother has explained your presence. I'll leave you both to it."

"Well, you *could* offer our guest something to drink, Rosalie," Kingsley said, somewhat impatiently.

"But, of course," Rosalie said, forcing a smile. "Fancy a cuppa, miss?"

"Oh, no, that's quite all right," Kori said.

"It's no problem. I have tea already made."

"Oh, no, please, I'm fine. Thank you, anyway."

Rosalie bowed slightly and left the room. For siblings who were supposed to be close, there was a sense of animosity in the air. What was that saying about guests and fish? Something about how they both begin to stink after a few days, Kori recalled. And Rosalie's brother had been there more than a few days.

Kori and Kingsley sat facing each other in the drawing room and Kingsley leaned in, saying in a low voice, "I must say, I miss my residence in Prince Grayson's manor."

"I'm sure you do, Mr. Moore."

"They won't let any of the servants back into the house until the prince is found. Please don't misunderstand. My sister is a good woman and a fine host, but, well, one gets used to one's own way of life, doesn't one?"

"Indeed."

"Now, how can I help you, Ms. Briggs? I must tell you that I've related to Agent Graham and everyone at MI5 all that I know. They were very thorough with their questioning and I like to think I was, in turn, very thorough with my answers."

"Yes, indeed you were, Mr. Moore. I've read the transcripts of your interviews. But there was scant information about the prince himself."

"The prince? I don't understand. He's missing, of course."

Kori chuckled. "Yes, so I've heard. No, what I mean is, about the prince as a person. I'd like to know a little something about him. It might help."

"Hmm, forgive me, but I'm not sure I'm following, Ms. Briggs."

"It's my methodology, Mr. Moore. Facts are good. Facts are necessary. But l like to go a little deeper. I like to understand the people involved in a case, both the perpetrators and the victims."

"I see." There was that skeptical look again.

"If you'll please indulge me, sir."

"Yes, yes," Kingsley said, shrugging. "If it would help."

"It would."

"Please fire away, Ms. Briggs."

"Well, first of all, you have stated that the prince arrived home on the night in question around midnight."

"That's correct. I heard a car pull up."

"From a place called White's, I believe?"

"Yes."

"And what's that?"

"White's? It's a famous gentlemen's club in St. James."

"A gentlemen's club? You mean . . . like, a strip club, sir?"

Kingsley burst out laughing. "Oh, my, Ms. Briggs, no, no, no. White's is a gentlemen's social club. A highly exclusive one. It was formed back in the late 1600s, you know. Very prestigious, and with a very distinguished membership."

Kori pictured it in her mind—men in silk suits smoking expensive cigars and drinking brandy in dark, leather chairs. Low lighting, deep pile carpeting, and floor-to-ceiling shelves filled with dusty old books that nobody ever reads.

"Does the prince go there often?"

"Oh, quite often. It's his favorite place to go, I would say, and, outside of royal occasions for which his position obligates his presence, his main venue of socialization."

"Does he go anywhere else?"

"Rarely."

"Does he talk about friends at this club of his? I mean, anybody in particular?"

"Well, it's no secret that his best friend at the club is Sir John Holland."

"The reclusive billionaire?"

"One and the same. They go way back, those two. They play cards all the time. And just between you and me, typically for pretty high stakes."

Kori continued asking questions about Prince Grayson's personal life, what little she gathered there was of it, until, finally, she reached the end of Kingsley's patience.

"Agent Briggs," he said at last. "I must ask, why all these questions? I fail to see how the prince's lifestyle will get us any closer to finding the prince and securing his safe release. Agent Graham asked none of these questions."

"Well, as I said, different investigators have different methods. I wouldn't be very useful if I came here and asked the same questions Agent Graham asked, would I? At any rate, I believe I have everything I need for now. You've been very patient and helpful and I appreciate your time, Mr. Moore."

"Well, if I was somehow of help, I am certainly glad of it."

Kori rose and headed for the door. Kingsley did likewise, beating her to it and opening it for her. As he did so, he surprised a young boy on the stoop who had his arm extended and was about to ring the bell. Like the young girl who'd left earlier, the boy, with crimson hair and freckles and rosy red cheeks, carried sheet music. Rosalie Shaw's next appointment had arrived.

Kingsley waved him in and turned to Kori. "Please do what you can," he said in a low voice. "I want very much to go home."

"I understand, Mr. Moore."

"I hope so, Ms. Briggs."

Kingsley closed the door and Kori found herself chuckling at the thought of the poor man having to listen to one cacophonous piano lesson after another. She walked two blocks to the intersection of a busy street and flagged down a cab. She didn't notice, nor would she have any reason to suspect, that a man in a dark suit was following about half a block behind her. The man watched as Kori got into her cab and as she did, he spoke into his cell phone. Kori's cab took off. A moment later, a dark sedan fell in line behind it.

**7**

—·—

Cooper had more trouble finding the butler and maid than he had tracking down Kingsley Moore. Charles and Violet Stewart had been servants to the prince for nineteen years but kept to themselves and seemingly had no friends or relatives in the London area. They rarely left the confines of their employer's manor house. Both were originally from Sheffield, about five hours north of the city, where they still had family, but according to the file, Victor Graham had ordered them not to leave the area.

In the back of the cab, Kori called Cooper, hoping he'd found something on the Stewarts while she'd been interviewing Kingsley Moore.

"Sorry, Kori," he said. "I got nothin'."

"Damn, Coop. What about hotels? I can tell you for sure that Kingsley Moore wishes he'd checked into one instead of staying with family."

"I ran their credit cards, but nothing shows up. They seem to have disappeared."

"Strange."

"Maybe they went back to Sheffield in defiance of Graham's order."

"That seems unlikely. After nineteen years of working for the prince, I can't imagine they wouldn't stick around during his disappearance."

"Is it so important that you find them?"

"Well, I'd like to at least talk to them. They might tell me something they forgot to tell MI5. You never know. Plus, we know that the butler always does it, right? I need to eliminate Charles Stewart as a suspect, plus his wife."

Cooper laughed. "Cozy mysteries aside, we already know who done it. Dempsey and this Burke guy. And I can find nothing on him, either, by the way. Of course, I'm sure they're lying pretty low."

"Of course."

Cooper was quiet for a moment and then said, "That's our focus, Kori, right? Finding Dempsey and Burke?"

"Sure, Coop."

"Wait a minute. You don't think so, do you?"

"I'm not sure what to think."

"Well, we've seen the photo, right? That's Dempsey, all smiles sitting next to Prince Grayson."

"I know."

"And the photo's authenticity has been confirmed by MI5's lab. And Burke flew to Boston and then flew back to London with Dempsey. I mean, it seems pretty straightforward, doesn't it?"

"Well, yes, but . . ." Kori's voice trailed off.

"But you think there's more to the story."

"Coop, there has to be. I don't know how to describe it, but Dempsey just doesn't feel right to me."

"Now you know I would never second-guess your instincts, Kori. On the other hand, the clock is kind of ticking, you know?"

"I know. But look, MI5 is all over the search for Burke. And they're scouring the city and the whole country for Dempsey. They don't need me for that. What good is one more person searching through the haystack going to do? What's needed is a different angle. I don't know what that angle is exactly, or what it's going to bring to the table, but I'm going to follow it. Somehow, I just know that this goes beyond what meets the eye."

"Well, what are you wasting time talking to me for, Kori? Get after it. You know you have our support. Just let us know what you need."

"Will do, Coop. Thanks."

Kori hung up and addressed the cab driver. "How much longer, sir?"

"About a half hour ma'am."

"Thank you."

The route from Hackney to Brixton, where the prince's private secretary Parker Bates lived and Kori's next destination, took her cab south over the river Thames and along streets where new buildings mixed with old. Kori gazed out of the window and wondered what she'd be doing if she were there as a tourist and not on a case.

First of all, she imagined she wouldn't be taking taxis to places. And not because of the cost, which would never be a factor anyway. Kori preferred to experience a city in a more engaging way. She'd walk. Or maybe she'd rent a bike. London was full of them. Most probably, she'd take the underground—the Tube, as it was known to Londoners. To where? Anywhere she wanted. She'd been to London several times and had never found a lack of things to do in any direction. It was a magnificent city. She'd see a show in one of the West End theaters, that would be a given. And there were countless museums to check out. Of course, she'd already done most of the standard tourist things. She'd taken a tour of the Tower of London, shopped and dined at Covent Garden, strolled through the National Gallery, seen St. Paul's Cathedral and Westminster Abbey, witnessed the changing of the guards at Buckingham Palace, and even crossed Abbey Road where the Beatles had crossed it for their iconic album cover.

For professional curiosity, Kori had once taken a Jack the Ripper tour in Whitechapel and imagined going back in time to solve the murders, confident that she could have. She fantasized about dressing up as a decoy prostitute, working the slums where the victims were all found, attracting the attention of the killer who remains unidentified to this day. Kori Briggs would have identified him and more.

Ah, but on this day, there was no time for tours and sightseeing and fantasies of solving long-cold crime cases. There was work to be done. And not much time to do it. Kori was keenly aware that there were but five days remaining to Dempsey's deadline. And the queen had no apparent plans to pay the ransom.

The cab driver pulled over in front of a nicely kept brick townhouse. Kori paid the fare and then, out of the corner of her eye, noticed a dark sedan swing around the cab, slowing down almost to a stop before speeding back up and going on its way down the street. It was as if the occupants of the vehicle were taking a long, close look at her. She was not exactly unaccustomed to being on the receiving end of an admiring—or lecherous—gaze from a man, but this seemed different somehow, less impulsive, more intentioned.

She leaned back into the cab. "Driver, did you happen to notice that dark sedan following us? The one that just passed by?"

"The one right up ahead? What about it, miss?"

"Had it been following us for long?"

"Oh, I really can't say, miss. I was more focused on where we were going than what was behind us. Sorry."

"No problem. Thank you."

"Have a nice day, miss."

Kori looked down the street to see the sedan make a turn at the next block. It was probably nothing, but Kori made a mental note all the same.

Parker Bates, fifty-three, was a tall, thin man with a narrow, pointed nose. He invited Kori into his townhouse after an initial conversation that was remarkably similar to Kori's conversation at the door with Kingsley Moore. So was the skepticism. This time, however, it helped that Kori could drop Moore's name. Once Bates knew that she'd talked at length to Moore, he not only invited her in, he insisted.

"So what did our good man Kingsley tell you about Prince Grayson?" Bates asked once he and Kori were seated in his small, tidy living room.

"Nothing at all, really," Kori said. "I didn't ask much about the prince. We talked mostly about the kidnapping itself. You know, the night in question and the following morning." It was a lie, but Kori wanted to see the reaction. It was subtle, but it looked like relief. *Interesting*, she thought.

"Yes, terrible business this kidnapping," Bates nodded. "Bloody terrible."

"And what do you do exactly for the prince, Mr. Bates?"

"I'm his private secretary, of course." Bates said it like it was universally known, like the whole world must know the name Parker Bates, although most people wouldn't be able to identify even the prince himself in a lineup.

"Yes, I understand, but what does being the private secretary entail exactly?"

"Well, I manage the prince's schedule, take his phone calls, deal with his correspondence, keep track of his finances, organize his travel itinerary, field questions from the press, that sort of thing."

"I see. So what kind of schedule does the prince keep?"

"What kind?"

"Yes, I mean, does he stay busy?"

"Oh, very. You see, Ms. Briggs, royalty is both a blessing and a curse. If you're a prince, you are seemingly wanted everywhere. There is always a speaking engagement. Schools, charitable institutions, trade unions, etcetera. And royal events are many and frequent. State banquets, dinner receptions, formal teas. And of course, the public is always looking for a statement about this or that. The paparazzi are ubiquitous. It's not a life for the shy and reserved, I'm afraid."

"No, I imagine it's not. What can you tell me about the prince's personal friends? Does he have any particularly close friends?"

"Hmm . . . not really. He has little time for personal relationships, you see."

"Girlfriend?"

Bates hesitated. "Not really."

"Not really?"

"No, Ms. Briggs, no girlfriend." Then he added, both playfully and awkwardly, "Are you interested in the position? The prince is famously single, you know."

Kori smiled and said, "Oh, I'm afraid I'm spoken for, Mr. Bates. My duty to my job is about all I can handle."

"Indeed."

"What can you tell me about the prince's friend, Sir John Holland?"

"What about him?"

"They're close, aren't they?"

"Is that what Moore told you?"

"I thought it was more or less common knowledge."

"Well, I'm sure Sir John would like to believe they are close chums. Everyone wants to be close to a prince, don't they? But, no, I do not believe that I would call them 'close.' I would not characterize the relationship in that way."

"What can you tell me about White's?"

"The club?"

"Yes, I understand the prince goes there quite regularly."

Bates chuckled. "Well, if you call once or twice a month 'regularly,' yes I suppose so. Indeed, he did spend the evening at White's on the night of the kidnapping, but it's hardly a place he frequents. Other obligations, of which there are many, as I've indicated, take precedence."

Kori asked a few more questions and then brushed up against Bates's patience as she had with Moore. *Just as well.* Kori felt as if she'd gotten everything she needed from Parker Bates, at least for the time being. Kori thanked him for his time and left.

Out on the street, she consulted the map on her phone to discover a pub a mere three blocks away. It was time for lunch. The Savoy Breakfast seemed like a long time ago. Kori ordered a burger and an Old Speckled Hen draft beer and thought about the interviews she'd had that morning, especially the differences in the answers she'd received.

Then she received a text. *My American friend, where are you? My plane was early. I am here, at the Savoy.*

Kori smiled. Anya! The presence of Rampart Agent Anya Kovalev meant that the investigation could proceed at least twice as fast, maybe faster, given that the sum was undoubtedly greater than the parts.

*Meet me in the Thames Foyer,* Kori texted back. *We'll have a spot of tea, as they say in these parts. I'll be there in a half hour.*

Kori wolfed down what was left of her lunch, paid the check, and went outside to hail a cab. Three minutes later, she was headed to the Savoy, a route that would take her over Westminster Bridge, which would cross the Thames and provide her a postcard view of the Palace of Westminster and Big Ben. But her plans changed when, in the back seat of the cab, she slowly turned around to see the same dark sedan following as before.

"Driver," she said, "I've changed my mind. Please take me to the Park Plaza hotel."

"Yes, ma'am. The Park Plaza hotel."

The Park Plaza overlooked the Thames, but the main street ran between it and the river. In front of the hotel, Kori paid the driver, observed the approaching sedan out of the corner of her eye, and then entered the lobby. She turned around and through the glass double doors, watched as the sedan slowed down and then stopped. Somebody got out. Kori hustled to the far end of the long lobby and took a seat in a chair that was partially hidden from the lobby doors by a building column. She waited for someone to enter after her. She didn't have to wait long. A minute later, a compact, muscular man, probably in his thirties, with black, slicked-back hair and wearing a dark, slim-fit suit that made him look even more muscular, strode into the lobby.

Kori peered out from behind the column, snapped a quick picture of the man with her phone, and then scurried off in the opposite direction, darting down a hallway that led to a couple of conference rooms. She found a stairwell and jogged two flights up, dashed down a hallway of guest rooms, took another stairwell down two flights to street level again, then found a side exit door. Now she was behind the hotel. She walked away from the river, then up two blocks along a major street where she found another cab. Fifteen minutes later, unencumbered by any would-be pursuers, she found herself back at the Savoy.

# 8

"I thought you said half an hour," Anya Kovalev said from her table at the Thames Foyer, the Savoy's glass-domed restaurant, famous for its afternoon tea service. In front of the petite but taut, athletic blond were finger sandwiches, scones, and, yes, tea.

"Yeah, sorry about that," said Kori, snatching a cucumber and cream cheese finger sandwich. "I had to stop and get rid of something on the way."

"So bring me up to speed, my American friend. It is no secret that the prince is missing. Chief Eaglethorpe briefed me on the ransom demand from one Newton Dempsey and his presumed partner-in-crime, Spenser Burke. Oh, and he also mentioned that you'd be buying the drinks."

"Yes, I suppose I did offer something like that as an enticement."

"It worked. Here I am."

"So you are. Well, so far I've been busy interviewing those closest to Prince Grayson, particularly those who were there when it was discovered he'd been kidnapped. His valet, Kingsley Moore, and his private secretary, Parker

Bates, specifically. No luck so far in tracking down the butler and maid, Charles and Violet Stewart. They seem to have fallen off the face of the earth.”

“But, Kori . . . what about finding, you know, the missing prince?”

“Hmm? The prince? Oh, I’m leaving that up to MI5.”

Anya burst out laughing.

“What’s so funny?” Kori asked.

“Oh, nothing. It is just such a ‘Kori Briggs’ thing to forgo the obvious. Rampart has been enlisted specifically to find Prince Grayson and yet you are off in another direction.”

“Yes, well—”

“It is not a criticism, my friend, believe me. Far from it. I have worked with you enough to know that you have your reasons for taking the investigative route you have taken. Reasons which you will now reveal to me and which, no doubt, I will find perfectly sensible. I am all ears, as they say.”

“Okay, well the reasoning is this: I don’t think Newton Dempsey is capable of pulling off a kidnapping such as this.”

“He is something of a genius if I understand correctly.”

“But London? A royal prince?”

“You forget his accomplice. This Burke fellow—”

“Nor do I think Dempsey has the interest in trying to pull off something like this.”

“I see.”

“Dempsey’s the wrong guy to be involved in this, Anya. Period.”

"But the photo . . ."

"I know, I know. I can't explain that. But something is amiss. There is more to this case. Much more."

"What does MI5 think?"

"How would I know? I gave them what I had on Dempsey, shared Burke's name with them, and then they kicked me to the curb like an old piece of furniture. They don't want our help. In fact, I think they're afraid we'll somehow get in the way. As it turns out, they're having me tailed. That's what I had to get rid of on the way here. Some MI5 guys have been following me since at least this morning. I lost them at the Park Plaza but it's not going to be hard for them to pick up the scent. They know I'm staying here at the Savoy, after all."

"Let them follow us," Anya said. "As long as they do not get in *our* way, what do we care?"

"Yeah, I guess so. It just irks me, you know?"

"Sure. Do you know anything about MI5's investigation thus far?"

"Well, the lead investigator was good enough to give me a copy of their case file, which I'm sure is probably only about fifty percent of what they've put together. My guess is that at this point, they're following every possible lead on Burke's whereabouts. Maybe they'll find him. And where he is, Dempsey probably is, and certainly the prince. They'll make a dramatic rescue and all will be right with the world. The prince will be returned and everyone will get medals. But when it's all said and done, I'll bet you a case of Scotch that they discover something that nobody saw coming."

"Such as?"

"I don't know. Another accomplice, perhaps? A skeleton in the prince's closet? Here's a thought: I think the prince may know his kidnappers. I think it's possible—no, *probable*—that there are more people involved than Dempsey and Burke."

"I have to admit that it does seem strange that Prince Grayson, of all the members of English royalty, would be the one kidnapped."

"Right? He's like the Zeppo of the group."

Anya laughed out loud. "Indeed," she said.

"Wait," said Kori, "you mean you got that? The Zeppo thing? I just used the phrase because the president used it and he and the chief had a good laugh about it. What does it mean?"

"Zeppo Marx?" said Anya. "You know, of the Marx Brothers? Everyone remembers Groucho, and most people remember Chico and Harpo, too. But Zeppo was the fourth. He was the straight man. Nobody remembers him."

"Aha," Kori smiled. "Okay, that makes sense. So how do you know so much about the Marx Brothers?"

"My father introduced me to them. He was a big fan. Of course, when he grew up, in the Soviet days, their movies were not available to us. But my father, being KGB, eventually had access to them. He introduced me to the Three Stooges, too."

"All the best of Western culture, huh?"

"You can learn a lot about America by its comedians."

"Hmm . . . never thought of it that way."

"But Kori, besides the strange choice of victim, why do you think Grayson might know his kidnappers?"

"No tangible reason. A hunch, I guess. I've been toying with the idea since this morning when Parker Bates gave me a completely different picture of the prince than what Kingsley Moore gave me. Something doesn't add up. Moore said he rarely goes anywhere, except to this specific gentleman's club, which he visits all the time."

"You mean, like a strip club?"

"I thought that's what he meant, too! No, apparently some hoity-toity men's social club called White's. Anyway, Bates said he only goes there a couple of times a month and that he's always busy attending various functions. Moore also said Grayson's best friend is Sir John Holland, the billionaire. Bates made it sound like the two hardly know each other. Both Moore and Bates work closely with the prince. It's clear that someone isn't being completely honest."

"Which one?"

"My bet would be Bates. Kingsley Moore seemed more genuine to me. Bates seemed to be trying to cover something. And he was keenly interested in knowing what Moore had told me."

"You think he's somehow involved in the kidnapping?"

"Doubtful. I don't believe it's an inside job, at least from those closest to the prince. It would be way too obvious. But it did get me thinking that it might be someone affiliated in some way with Grayson. I'd love to talk to Sir John Holland, for instance. He clearly has no financial motive, so he's obviously an unlikely suspect, but maybe he knows someone, someone he wouldn't suspect himself, but maybe someone who's also worth talking to. I'd also love to know what Bates knows, and I mean what he *really* knows. And I'd love to know a heck of a lot more about the prince's personal life. Plus, there's still the butler and maid to talk to."

"So it seems we have much to do. What first?"

"Want to go to a gentlemen's club?"

"Only if it's the—how did you say?—the hoity-toity kind."

"That it is, Anya. Come on, let's see if we can get there without being followed by the MI5 pinheads."

White's was a twenty-minute walk from the Savoy, which took the agents along the Strand, through Trafalgar Square, where they blended in with the crowds of tourists and locals alike, past theaters, down Piccadilly, and to St. James's Street, where White's was located in a five-story Victorian stone building with a Palladian facade. At no point along the way did the agents notice anybody following them.

The history of the building that housed White's dated to 1674; the history of White's to 1693, making it the oldest club in London. It was one of the last men-only clubs in the UK, a point that perpetually rankled the women of the city and, in fact, inwardly rankled both Kori and Anya, though neither could imagine any possible reason to want to belong. Grayson's brother, Prince Charles, and nephew, Prince William, were also members of the club and, in fact, Prince Charles had his bachelor party at White's before marrying Lady Diana Spencer. One's imagining of the level of debauchery at the bachelor party would certainly be tempered, however, upon learning that among those in attendance that night was Queen Elizabeth herself, the club making a rare exception to their policy and allowing a woman to be present. Why Charles insisted that his mother attend his bachelor party remains a peculiar mystery to this day.

"There's no sign on the door," Anya observed as they approached the club.

"Not surprising," said Kori. "London's most exclusive club. It's not like they're looking for publicity."

"Should we just knock?"

"Might as well. What have we got to lose? What are they going to do, not let us in?"

The agents walked up the steps from the street and Kori rapped on the black wooden door. Presently, an older, slim man with narrow eyes and wearing a dark suit opened the door a crack and peered out.

"Yes?" the man said.

"Is this White's?" Kori asked.

"Yes. May I help you?"

"Sir, we're US agents investigating the disappearance of the prince. We know he's a member here and we'd like to ask some questions." Kori showed the man her National Bureau of Criminal Investigations ID.

"I see. And why would US agents be investigating a British prince?" the man said.

The disappearance of the prince was common knowledge. The fact that he was presumably kidnapped, and by an American, was not. Kori had to tread carefully.

"We've been asked to join the investigation at the request of the prime minister," she replied. "I'm not at liberty to say why. Your cooperation, sir, would be greatly appreciated." Then she figured she'd try the same tack she used with Kingsley Moore. "You're welcome to call Agent Victor Graham if you'd like to substantiate our presence here."

"I don't know who that is."

"He's the lead investigator. With MI5?"

The man looked back at Kori blankly.

"Surely," she said, "someone from MI5 has been here about the matter of the prince's disappearance."

"I'm afraid not, miss."

"Are you here a lot, sir?"

"I should say so. I am the steward. My name is Edwards."

"And nobody from MI5 has come by to interview any of the members, Mr. Edwards?"

"No, miss. Nobody has been interviewed."

"I see. Well, I suppose they've left that up to us then. May we come in?"

"Oh, I'm afraid that would be quite impossible, miss. I'm not at liberty to allow non-members into the building, no matter their business, unless they have been specifically invited by a member. Or, in the case of law enforcement, have some sort of a warrant."

Anya couldn't resist. "Do you get law enforcement officers here a lot, Mr. Edwards?" she asked.

Edwards ignored the question. "Moreover," he continued, "I'm not at liberty to disclose who is or who is not present within this building at any given time. If there is a specific member you wish to question, I would suggest you question them at their home or place of business. I'm sorry I can't be of more help."

"May we at least leave word with you that we're looking for information on the prince's disappearance?" Kori said. "If anyone has anything to offer, they can contact us. No matter how insignificant their information might seem to be. Anything could help. We all want a happy resolution, don't we, Mr. Edwards?"

Edwards stood mute for a moment and then said, "I suppose I could pass the word. Leave your card with me. I'll make inquiries, although I'm quite certain that if anybody in the club knew anything, they would certainly have come forward by now. Where can one reach you?"

"Thank you, Mr. Edwards," said Kori. "We can be reached at the Savoy."

"Very good, miss." Edwards took Kori's card, nodded curtly, and closed the door.

"What do you suppose goes on in there?" Kori asked Anya, looking at the closed door.

"Probably nothing," Anya replied. "But the secret with an exclusive club like this is to stoke the mystery. Like a good striptease artist."

"Emphasis on *tease*."

"Exactly. Nobody knows what goes on, but everyone wants to join."

The two turned and began making their way back to the hotel.

"Anya, don't you find it strange that MI5 hasn't bothered to visit the club?" Kori asked.

"Not at all," Anya replied.

"Really? I do."

"That's because you are thinking like Kori Briggs, my friend. Think of it from MI5's perspective. The prince disappeared from his chambers, not from here. They were busy combing the grounds, looking for clues at the scene of the crime. Once the ransom note came in, they knew, in their minds, who the kidnapper was. Your discovery of his accomplice gave them the final piece of their puzzle. The mystery was solved. Now their work is clear to them. Find Dempsey, find Burke, find the prince. White's is no concern to them."

"Hmm . . . I suppose you're right. I suppose it was also too much to expect that we'd be allowed in. And much too much to expect that we'd be able to question someone like Sir John Holland. He could have been in there, for all we know. And I'll be shocked if anybody reaches out to us, assuming Edwards even passes along our information."

"Agreed."

"Well, you know what? I'm getting tired of knocking on doors for information. I feel like a door-to-door vacuum cleaner salesman. And one who's having a bad day. We need more information about the prince to determine who's really involved in the kidnapping, and I've had a feeling ever since I talked to him this morning that Bates has some answers he's not giving. I've seen his home, now I want to see his office."

"Where is it?"

"In the prince's manor."

"Oh, boy, I think I see where this is heading."

"Tonight, Anya. Let's pay a no-knock visit to the manor tonight. Just you and me and your glass cutter. No invitation necessary. And nobody to close a door in our faces. Then, maybe we can get somewhere."

**9**

Dinner at the Savoy was poached oysters, smoked haddock in aged cheddar sauce, and apple tarte Tatin. Drinks included something called a Lauren Bacall, vodka mixed with maraschino liqueur and hibiscus bitters.

Sufficiently fortified, the agents dressed in black and took a cab to Regent's Park, within walking distance of the prince's manor. They hiked a circuitous route from there, still cognizant of the fact that someone from MI5 might be following, and crept up a dark alley behind the large, Gothic-revival style mansion. They knew that out in front of the manor there were paparazzi as well as guards.

From behind some bushes, they could see that the rear of the manor was not as well-attended. The half-moon provided some light, as did a street lamp at the corner of the property. Two bored-looking bobbies were patrolling along the rear alley. Kori was formulating some kind of diversion when one of the bobbies trotted around the side of the house apparently to relieve himself behind some shrubbery. That left a single guard who strolled toward the agents, stopped, lit a cigarette, then turned and strolled in the other direction.

"Here's our chance," Kori whispered. A low brick wall surrounded the property and a tall hedge ran beyond that. Kori and Anya clambered over the wall easily enough, but the dense hedge was another story. They crept along the hedge until, somewhere around the side of the manor opposite where the first bobby had retreated, they spied a small gap with just enough space to squeeze through.

"The MI5 report said none of the neighbors saw anything that night," Kori whispered. "Now I can see why. Walls and hedges are good for discouraging trespassers, but they also make it easy to stay hidden from sight. Come on."

The pair slipped through the hedge and then, on hands and knees, regarded the manor before them. "Where to now?" Anya whispered. "Do you know the floor plan?"

"Yes, there was a sketch in the report. And of course, I was led to Grayson's chambers on the third floor. I think that window straight ahead is the billiard room. Bates's office is actually on the other side of the house, but this might be as good a place as any to enter. We sure can't go around to the front."

"How do we overcome the alarm system?"

"Good question. It was off the night the prince was kidnapped, but I assume they've reactivated it by now. Think the windows are wired?"

"Probably. It's the home of a prince."

"What about the second-floor windows? Nobody ever thinks about wiring the second-floor windows. And certainly not the third, which, now that I think about it, is probably why Dempsey and Burke chose to use a ladder that night. I'll bet you another Lauren Bacall that the upstairs windows are clear."

"That only leaves the question of how to get up there, Kori. Unlike the kidnappers, we do not have a ladder."

"Ah, but check out the trellis over there," Kori whispered, pointing beyond the billiard room windows to an ivy-covered wooden framework along the exterior wall of the house about forty feet from them. "We can climb up that. Just as good as a ladder, no?"

"Except that it does not reach the second floor, Kori. It stops short of the window above it by a good five feet."

"Yes, but the window has a ledge. We can pull ourselves up. Easy peasy."

Anya looked dubious but had no alternative to offer. "Okay, my friend. Lead on."

"Let's stay close to the ground and move slowly," Kori suggested.

The two crawled along the grass lawn until they made it to the trellis.

"After you," whispered Kori.

"I don't think so," Anya said with a chuckle. "You are much taller. I will have trouble reaching the ledge. You are going to have to go first and then pull me up."

"Fair enough, my Russian friend. But the ledge can't be more than a foot deep. I'll need to be in the room, leaning over the edge from the inside to grab your hands to pull you up. That means I'll need the glass cutter."

"Of course."

Kori took the cutter from Anya and climbed up the trellis. Balancing precariously on the top of it, she raised her hands above her head, gripped the ledge of the window, and thanked her lucky stars that she spent so much time working out. The maneuver was essentially a long pull-up made more difficult because she couldn't grip the ledge like a pull-up bar; most of the pulling had to come from her fingers along the top of the ledge. She was at least helped by the fact that she could push her boot into the stone wall she was facing to give her some leverage. Eventually, she raised herself enough to swing a knee up on the ledge and the rest of her body followed. She stood slowly. With only a foot of depth, she had to press herself flat against the window. She fumbled in her pocket for the glass cutter, almost dropping it before getting a good handle on it. Then she used it to trace a circle in the glass above the window lock. She popped out the cut piece, unlatched the window, and slid it upward from the bottom. She hesitated, listening for the sound of an alarm but there was only silence.

She stepped into what appeared to be an unused bedroom. She crossed the room and stole a quick glance out into the dark hallway. All was quiet. Then she went back to the window, leaned out, and waved Anya up. Anya negotiated the trellis with little difficulty, then stood atop of it reaching upward. Kori leaned over as far as she could, grabbed Anya's hands, and pulled. Anya pushed her foot against the wall as Kori had done and was soon climbing over the ledge and into the bedroom.

"Thanks for the lift," she whispered.

"No charge. And you owe me a Lauren Bacall."

"Noted."

"Come on. Bates's office is on the first floor, right off the foyer."

The two exited the bedroom into the hallway and noticed an adjacent spiral staircase. Both agents used the flashlight on their phones to navigate the steps down to the first floor. At the bottom, they found themselves in a small anterior room with heavy, stuffed chairs, a tall cabinet, and a long mahogany desk. Through the anterior room was a round, cavernous room with a grand piano on one side and some tables and chairs scattered around the periphery.

"Ballroom," Kori said. "I've been thinking of putting one in my place."

"Yes," Anya nodded. "What home is complete without one?"

"The office is on the far side of this floor. I guess we go through that door," Kori said, pointing to a door at the other end of the room.

"What about that door?" Anya said, pointing to a closer door that presumably went off in a different direction. "Or that one over there?"

"Hmm . . ." Kori mused, glancing about the circular room. "I don't remember seeing all these doors in the floor plan. I'm just figuring the farthest one should get us closer to the other end of the house, right?"

"Proceed," Anya said. "I am only pointing out options."

They walked across the ballroom and opened the far door to find nothing but darkness. Kori pointed her flashlight ahead of her to discover that they had wandered into a large storage area, complete with rows of folded chairs and stacks of long tables, but no means of egress other than the door through which they'd entered.

"This storage room is bigger than my apartment," Kori remarked. "I'll bet none of this stuff is ever used. From what I understand, Grayson is the last guy you'd expect to throw some kind of ball. Okay, let's try one of your other options."

The agents walked back to the nearer door and found a hallway on the other side of it.

"This looks more promising," said Anya.

The hallway led into one of the several drawing rooms of the house, this one decorated in the manner of a seventeenth-century French villa, complete with Louis fourteenth giltwood carved armchairs and baroque-style cabinets and moldings. There was low-level illumination from recessed wall lights that the agents would discover was prevalent throughout the manor, thus giving them enough light to see. They turned their phone flashlights off.

Through the drawing room was a small, narrow lounge with a long bar, bar stools, and a mirrored wall behind a long shelf of liquor bottles.

"Finally," said Kori. "A room with some kind of practical function."

Through the bar was another drawing room, this one in 1930s art deco style, and beyond that was a short hallway that led into what appeared to be the foyer of the house—a large open area with a marble tile floor and a tall chandelier hanging from the high ceiling. A double staircase led to the second floor and wide double doors led out to the large porch at the front of the manor.

"Looks like we made it to the other side," said Kori. "Bates's office is here somewhere. There. That door on the other side of the staircase. That's it."

The agents stepped across the foyer, entered the room, and closed the door behind them. Kori flipped on the light switch.

"It's his office all right," she said. A large oak desk rested in the middle of the room with a hutch against the far wall with shelves that held pictures of Parker Bates and his family, plus a few of Bates with the prince, one of them apparently taken at Buckingham Palace with the queen.

"Wonder how you get to be a private secretary to a prince," Kori said.

"You probably have to know someone."

"Yeah, probably."

"So what are we looking for?" said Anya.

"Great question. Who knows? Anything that might tell us something about the kidnappers, I guess. You check out the desk drawers. I'll go through this cabinet."

Anya began rifling through the drawers, finding very little of interest, but Kori came upon a ledger. She opened it to see columns of numbers. "Anya, what can you make of this?" she said. "You studied accounting in college, right?"

"Architecture."

"Whatever. Take a look."

Anya grabbed the ledger and leafed through the pages, coming to the most recent entries. "Well, my friend, one does not need to be a CPA to notice something strange here."

"Like what?"

"Like the brackets around the bottom number. Meaning that it is negative. By much. See? This is apparently the record of some kind of financial account. Maybe the prince's personal bank account."

"So you're saying he's overdrawn?"

"Maybe. But nobody would allow someone, royalty or not, to be *this* overdrawn. There are no notations as to what kind of account this is. For all we know, it is one of many. A man like the prince might have several personal and investment accounts. But whatever it is, it was big at one time. Look up here." Anya pointed to an entry dated six months earlier: £452,156.

"Pretty healthy," Kori said.

"Yes, now look at the most recent entry."

"*Minus* £632,980? Wow. A swing of over a million pounds. That's a lot of money to lose. But you're right, Anya. How does a single account go so negative? No financial institution would allow that. Do you think it's some kind of business venture gone bad?"

"Maybe. The point is, he owes somebody over six hundred thousand pounds."

"This is getting interesting. Let's keep looking."

The agents continued poring through the paperwork in Bates's office until, finally, Anya came across a large, dark-brown manila envelope with a string closure. She unwound the string and pulled out numerous pages stapled together in the corner. "Bingo," she said.

Kori dropped the file folder she was leafing through. "What have you found?"

"A promissory note. Or notes, I should say. A stack of them." Anya sat in the chair behind the desk and grabbed a calculator and began punching away as she flipped through the stack of pages. "It adds up," she said at last. "632,980 pounds."

"So who are the notes from?"

Anya read the letterhead. "JEH Financial Group, 23 Queen Victoria Street, London."

"So if you're a prince, I guess you can just waltz into the offices of a major lending company and borrow whatever you need. Repeatedly."

"Well, he *is* royalty. I suppose his credit is pretty good."

"Yeah, I suppose. But why so much debt? What's the prince spending so much money on? The guy doesn't go anywhere. In fact, he—"

"Shhh!" said Anya. "Kori, listen."

Above them came the sound of footsteps on hardwood flooring. Kori darted over to the door and hit the light. The agents listened in the dark as the sound of one set of footsteps became two.

"We're not alone," Kori whispered, looking at the ceiling.

"But who would be in the house?" Anya whispered back. "It is cordoned off as a crime scene."

"That didn't stop us."

"True."

"Well, there's only one way to find out." Kori pulled out her Glock.

"Wait, Kori, maybe it's MI5 reviewing the crime scene again. We would be arrested."

"Yes, I suppose you're right. Still, we need to know for sure. And if it is MI5, I'd like to know what they're back here for. What are they hoping to find that they haven't already found? And at this time of night? We've got the advantage. They don't know we're here. Come on, let's sneak up the staircase and do a little spying on the spies."

# 10

—·—

The agents slipped out of Bates's office and crept up the double staircase. At the second-floor landing, they looked down the dark hallway to see light coming from one of the bedrooms. They froze and could hear two people talking softly, a man and a woman.

They continued down the hallway. Kori flattened her back against the wall and inched up to the door. She quickly poked her head around the door jamb to get a glimpse of the intruders and then pulled herself back.

"Not MI5," she whispered. "Let's find out what their business here is."

"Right."

Kori spun into the room holding her Glock in front of her. Anya was right behind with her Sig Sauer.

"Hands up!" said Kori. "Police."

A man, probably in his sixties, portly, with white hair and a stunned expression, and a woman, same age, lean, with dark hair tied in a bun and an equally surprised look on her face, raised their hands up high.

"Who are you?" Kori asked. "And what are you doing here?"

"Don't shoot," said the man. "We're not robbing the place. I swear. We live here, you see."

Kori lowered her weapon. "Charles and Violet Stewart, I presume."

"Yes, ma'am." Then he took a closer look at the two agents, each dressed in black, the one having spoken aloud in an American accent. "Are you really with the police?" he asked.

"Sort of. We're American intelligence agents, investigating the prince's disappearance in conjunction with MI5." This was close enough to the truth. She showed them her ID. "You two disappeared too, you know. I think the last place anybody expected you to be would be here. This house is closed, or didn't you hear?"

"We've got no place else to go, ma'am," Violet Stewart said, lowering her hands. "And this is our home. Everything we have is here. We snuck back in after the crime scene people all left."

"How did you get in past the guards?"

Violet looked at Charles who shrugged. "Might as well tell 'em," he said.

"Secret passage," said Violet.

"Secret passage?"

"Yes, ma'am. Underground. All these rich old houses have them. Left over from the war, you know. To keep the occupants safe from the bombs of the German Luftwaffe. The passage comes out across the alleyway in the back. The exit looks like an ordinary sewer grate from above."

"Who else knows about this passage?"

"Just the prince, I suppose," said Charles. "It's never used, of course. Bloody damp and dark, it is. I'd almost forgotten about it. It'll be nice when this whole thing blows over and we can come and go as we please again through the servants' door."

"Aye, never was a truer word spoke," said Violet. "Can you tell us, ma'am, anything about the prince? Are you any closer to finding him?"

"I'm afraid not," Kori replied. She glanced about the room. It was more than a bedroom. The room they were standing in was a small living room with an adjoining kitchenette. Through the living area was the bedroom, as Kori remembered from the floor plan. But the door to the bedroom was closed. Of course it was. The bedroom had windows. The living area did not, hence, the fact that the floor lamp was on. Nobody from the street could tell anybody was there.

"So, you mean to tell us that you have been here since the kidnapping?" asked Anya.

"Yes, ma'am," said Charles. "As the missus said, we really have no place else to go. Hotels are so expensive. I suppose you'll be turning us in, but we meant no harm. Truly we didn't."

"Mind if I look around?" said Kori.

"Be our guest," said Violet.

"Anya, use your flashlight and keep it on these two." Kori switched off the floor lamp and then opened the bedroom door, using her phone's flashlight but being careful not to point it toward the window. She glanced around, opened up the closet, looked under the bed, and checked the bathroom. Then she came back out into the living area, closed the bedroom door behind her, and flipped the lamp back on.

"Well, there's no prince in there," she said.

"Begging your pardon, miss?" said Charles.

"Sorry. We need to rule you out as suspects."

"Kidnap the prince?" Violet said. "That would be the day!"

"Listen, Mr. and Mrs. Stewart, it doesn't matter to us that you're here, but you could get yourselves into serious trouble with your government. Let me make you a deal. Answer some questions for us and we'll get you to a hotel, all expenses paid. Fair enough?"

"You'd do that for us?" asked Violet with a trace of a smile.

"Yes," Kori replied.

Violet looked at Charles who smiled and nodded. "I do have to say, it's been stressful living here," he said. "Neither one of us has slept very well. We've been expecting at any moment that someone would discover us. We'll help all we can, but I have to tell you that we've told MI5 all that we know about the kidnapping."

"Which isn't much," said Violet. "We didn't hear a thing that night, you see. It wasn't until Kingsley discovered the prince was missing that we knew anything about it at all."

"Yes," said Kori, "I've read your interview. We'd like to ask you some questions about the prince himself, actually."

"The prince himself?" said Charles.

"Yes."

"Well, certainly. If it'll help."

"Thank you. By the way, my name is Kori and this is my associate Anya."

"Where are our manners?" said Violet. "Please sit down, ladies. Spot of tea? It's already made."

"That would be lovely," said Kori.

"Yes, please," Anya nodded. "If it's no trouble."

"'Tis no trouble at all, ma'am."

Violet served the tea while everyone took a seat. Kori glanced over and noticed the Stewart's small TV was tuned to BBC News, although the sound had been turned down. She could see that it was yet another report about the prince's disappearance.

"The TV," she said.

"Oh, yes, how rude," said Charles, reaching for the remote. "Here, let me turn that off."

"No, no, I was going to ask you to turn it up."

"Up? Of course."

The newscaster was speaking of a "person of interest." Onto the screen came a picture of Newton Dempsey.

"Look, Anya," said Kori. "MI5 must be getting desperate in their search for leads. Showing a person of interest is tantamount to admitting to the public that foul play was involved. Now watch the rumors fly. Okay, thank you, Charles. You can turn it off now."

Charles pointed the remote at the screen but nothing happened. "Bloody TV," he said. "Nothing ever works right with this old thing. Maybe one of these days, we'll get a new one. A nice big one."

"Where would we ever get the money?" Violet sighed.

Finally, the remote did its job and the screen went black. "Now, ladies, what would you like to know?" Charles asked.

Kori asked questions similar to what she'd asked Kingsley Moore and Parker Bates, the answers lining up more consistently with the answers Moore had given. The prince rarely went out, and when he did, it was typically to White's, and his best friend in the world seemed to be Sir John Holland.

"Did he have any other friends or visitors?" Kori asked.

Charles and Violet exchanged glances and Violet said, "No, not really."

The glance between the two of them was not lost on Kori. "No?" she said. "Are you sure?"

"Well," said Charles, "now that I think about it, recently, there was a visitor who came around on two occasions. Prince Grayson had him invited in and both times, they retreated to the prince's suite."

"Did you know who he was?"

"No, ma'am. We'd never seen him before."

"Did he identify himself?"

"Yes, he called himself Quincy, though I don't know whether that was his first or last name. Now let's see, on both occasions, as I recall, I answered the door and he said, 'Tell your master that Quincy is here to see him.' And on both occasions, the prince ordered me to send him right up."

"Interesting. Did you mention this to MI5?" Kori asked.

"No, ma'am. It hadn't occurred to me," Charles said a bit guiltily. "It was several days before the disappearance and I didn't really put it together. I suppose we should have mentioned something, but Agent Graham asked mostly about the night in question. I'll call him first thing in the morning if you think it's important."

"No, don't bother," Kori said. "I'll call him myself."

"Very good, ma'am."

"Could you describe this Quincy person?" Anya asked.

"Well, let me think. Well-built young man. In his thirties, I would say. Wouldn't you say so, dear?"

"Yes, that's about right," Violet chimed in. "Black hair, all slicked back."

"And well-dressed," Charles added. "Always a suit. Tight-fitting, the way they're wearing them these days, you know."

The description rang a bell. Could it be? Kori took out her phone and showed the couple the photo of the man in the lobby of the Park Plaza hotel who had been following her.

"Yes, that's him," said Charles. "Do you know him?"

"I thought I did," said Kori. "But apparently he's not who I imagined him to be."

The Stewarts showed Kori and Anya out of the manor property through the secret passageway, a dark, narrow tunnel accessed from the ballroom that led them outside to within ten yards of where the agents had initially stood behind the bushes. All four managed to ascend the short, steel ladder at the end of the tunnel. Kori went first, sliding the grate out of the way and poking her head up to make sure nobody was around. The angle from across the alley and obscured by a tall, wide elm tree, made them invisible to the bobbies in the back garden of the manor. Charles came up next, then Violet with Anya spotting her from below. Up on ground level again, Violet brushed off the front of her clothes and whispered, "I'm glad we won't be having a need to do that again!"

The four walked three blocks away from the manor to the main road. Kori waved down a taxi and they all rode to a nearby hotel where Kori checked the Stewarts in.

"Thank you again," Charles said. "I think tonight, we'll finally get a good night's sleep."

It was midnight by the time Kori and Anya made it back to the Savoy and ordered a nightcap at the hotel's famed American Bar. The agents were sitting in polished leather club chairs at a small table near a window. Kori was working on her customary Scotch, Anya her customary vodka. The piano player was working on a light jazz tune.

"Kori," said Anya, "you have to tell MI5 what you learned about this Quincy person."

"Do I?"

"Of course you do. They have a right to know. It might help with their investigation. This is not the kind of information we can keep to ourselves."

"I know, I know. It's just that I'm still a little sore about the snub."

"I understand. But, Kori, think about it. Maybe you can do a quid pro quo. By now, they must have some information we can use, right?"

"Maybe. I mean, I would think so."

"You give them Quincy with the understanding that they toss a little information our way. Or, at the very least, let us use them to identify who Quincy is for us. That would be fair, no?"

Kori mulled it over, took a swig of her Scotch, then pulled out her phone, dialing MI5 agent Victor Graham's number.

"Agent Briggs," Graham said.

"Hope I didn't wake you, Agent Graham," said Kori.

"Not at all. We're all working overtime, aren't we?"

"Indeed we are. Listen, I have some information that I think might be of interest to you."

"Oh? Do go on, Agent Briggs."

"Nuh-uh. Not over the phone. Let's meet in the morning. You can buy me breakfast."

"Breakfast, Agent Briggs?"

"Yes, and that's just one of my conditions. The other is that I need to know what you guys know."

"I gave you the file, Agent Briggs."

"Come on, Graham. I mean the stuff that's not in the file. I'll bet there's a ton of it. Now please don't make me call my superior who will, in turn, call the president who will, in turn, call your prime minister who will, in turn, wonder why you're not cooperating with us the way you're supposed to."

Graham was silent for a moment. Finally, he said, "This information had better be good. Agent Briggs."

"Trust me, it is. You're going to want to know what I know."

"Very well then. Breakfast. There's a place near your hotel called Deacon's Bistro that serves a proper British breakfast. You know, a traditional fry-up with bangers and black pudding and so forth. Shall we say eight?"

"I'll be there, Agent Graham."

Kori hung up and turned to Anya. "Breakfast at eight," she said. "Bangers and black pudding and so forth."

"Huh?"

"You know, a proper British breakfast."

"I see."

"Anyway, it'll be interesting to see how it goes."

"Very."

The two remained silent for a minute or so, both mulling the case and listening to the piano player. Outside, it began to rain.

"I wondered when we'd see rain," Kori remarked. "It's been far too sunny for England."

"Nothing falls like London rain," Anya said, looking out of the window into the drizzly night.

"So I've heard." Then Kori took a sip of her Scotch and said, "So, Anya, we haven't really had a chance to talk."

"No, we haven't, my friend."

"Well, I have to ask you how Moscow is these days."

"Crazy, I am afraid."

"Yes, I assumed as much."

"All of Russia is crazy. I do not, for the life of me, understand the direction in which the country is being led. Russia is now a pariah state. And for what? I would leave if my presence wasn't needed there for Rampart."

"We need eyes on the situation, Anya."

"Yes, I know it is my duty. My contacts at the Kremlin have been helpful."

"That's what Director Eaglethorpe tells me. I know you've been funneling information to the Joint Chiefs of Staff. Be careful, Anya. The Russian leadership is insane. I worry about you."

"Thank you. I will."

"And how is Nikolai?"

"Ah, Nikolai," Anya said wistfully.

"Uh-oh. Something tells me things aren't good."

"They are worse than not good. They are over, I am afraid."

"Oh, Anya, I'm sorry."

"It is okay."

"You let him down easy, I hope."

"As best I could." She was quiet for a moment before adding, "It could never work, you know."

"Yes," Kori nodded. "I know."

Anya looked down at her empty glass, then her gaze went back to the window. Kori struggled for something to say, eventually settling on the only appropriate words there were for the situation. "Another round, my friend?"

**11**

— · —

The smoky, gray eyes weren't any less enticing, but Kori kept focused.

"His name is Quincy," she said, showing Graham the picture on her phone. She had come to Deacon's Café alone, figuring Graham might be more open with just her, rather than with her and Anya. The two were seated in a booth by a window. The rain from the night before had stopped, but the skies were overcast. Anya, meanwhile, was back at the hotel on her laptop, sending a current progress report to Rampart HQ.

"I'll forward you this pic," Kori continued.

"Don't bother, Agent Briggs," said Graham, sprinkling some salt on his fried eggs. "We already know about Quincy."

"You do?"

"Yes. He's a nobody."

"He's apparently a friend of Grayson's, Agent Graham. He's visited him twice, in fact. In private, in the prince's living quarters. Both times were very recent."

"And how do you know this, Agent Briggs?"

"I'm an investigator remember? I investigated."

"I see. Well, as it turns out, Quincy's presence at the manor is easily explained," said Graham, lifting a forkful of eggs to his mouth.

"Yes?"

Graham hesitated, taking the time to chew and swallow the mouthful of food. Finally, he continued. "Yes, Quincy is an employee at White's, you see. The private club?"

"Yes, I know all about White's."

"Well, he's a private security officer of sorts. Grayson got wind of his potential kidnapping. Quincy went to see him to double-check the security of his quarters. And that's really all there is to that."

"Uh-huh. So why is this guy Quincy following me around?"

"Who knows? Have you been to White's?"

"Of course."

"Well, there you are then. They probably decided to have you followed from there. They're very careful."

"Except that Quincy was following me before I visited White's."

"Well, they discovered you somehow. White's takes care of their own. I really have no clue as to how their security operates, to be honest with you, Agent Briggs. It's not my department. You'll have to ask them how they came upon your presence here and why they're following you."

"So you're saying you've talked to this Quincy."

"Of course."

"And how did Grayson 'get wind' of the kidnapping?"

"Quincy tells us that on a couple of occasions, the prince felt he was being followed from the club. So, Quincy was sent out to do a security check."

"He didn't do a very good job."

"No, I daresay he didn't, did he?"

"And how did you find out about Quincy?"

"Through interviews at White's, of course."

"You interviewed people at White's personally?"

"Well, of course, Ms. Briggs."

"So you met the steward, Mr. Jenkins," Kori said, throwing out a fake name.

"Yes, of course, I met Mr. Jenkins."

"Uh-huh. You know, maybe I'll just go back to White's and see if I can talk to this Quincy myself."

"Won't do you any good, Agent Briggs. They're very secretive at White's. I imagine they'll deny he's even employed there."

"What's Quincy's full name?"

Graham took a long sip of his tea. "Andrew. Andrew Quincy. Now, listen, Agent Briggs, if that's all you have to give me, I'm afraid I'll have to be going."

"Now wait a minute, Agent Graham. You promised to share some information with me."

"Well, yes, but the deal was that you had something we could use. And you clearly don't. If it's any consolation, Agent Briggs, this lovely breakfast is on me. There. I believe we're now even."

"Look, Agent Graham, I know you've got your panties in a wad over the fact that your PM brought in some extra help. You're resentful. I get that. Nevertheless, I'm here.

And I'm not going away, so you might as well accept that. You might find this hard to believe, but my agency may actually be an asset for you. We've solved a case or two in our time. American intelligence is the best in the world."

"Debatable, Agent Briggs. I'll put MI5 up against anyone. And our international agency? MI6? The cream of the world's intelligence crop. We've got James Bond, after all."

"I'm sorry, who?"

"It doesn't matter, Ms. Briggs. I have no doubt you mean well, but I really don't see how you can help us. You've been very good about getting us the name of Spenser Burke and I've expressed our appreciation for that. But we are quite capable of handling things without your participation."

"Oh? So where *is* Burke?"

"We're looking for him, Agent Briggs, I assure you."

"Uh-huh. And Newton Dempsey?"

"What is your point, Ms. Briggs?"

"My point is you could use some help. Do you know where the Stewarts are right now?"

"No. Why?"

"Did you know about Prince Grayson's debts?"

"His debts, Agent Briggs?"

"That's what I thought. Listen, Graham, if you ever get serious about your so-called investigation, you know where to find me." Kori reached into her purse and drew out a fifty-pound note. Rising from her seat, she tossed it on the table. "For breakfast, Agent Graham," she said, and then she strode out of the café.

"He's top-shelf," Agent Darren Cooper said. "Twenty-five years with the agency, numerous decorations including medals from the queen herself for gallantry and distinguished service."

Kori was back at the Savoy in Anya's room. She'd briefed Anya on the fruitless breakfast meeting and then decided to call Cooper to dig a little deeper into Agent Victor Graham of MI5.

"Really, Coop? I find that all hard to believe."

"Kori, there's a reason he's heading up the investigation into the prince's kidnapping. You think they'd put someone in charge without the chops to solve the case? It's the prince, for God's sake."

"I know, I know. But I'm telling you, Coop, something doesn't sit right with me about the guy."

"I can't find a thing wrong with him. No reprimands, no censures, not a single black mark in his file. You know that I think, Kori? I think you're just pissed that he won't cooperate with you."

Kori sighed. "Maybe."

"Screw him," said Cooper. "You and Anya don't need MI5. Keep doing what you're doing. I have a feeling that when this is all over, he's going to be apologizing to you."

"I wouldn't hold my breath, Coop."

"Either way, remember—the clock is ticking. You're down to four days, Kori."

"I know. Okay, well thanks for checking into him, Coop. Sorry to bother you so early. What time is it there, anyway?"

"Four a.m."

"Yikes. I owe you a beer."

"And I plan on collecting."

Kori hung up and turned to Anya. "Well, Coop vouches for the guy's authority and credibility. But I can read people, Anya. His whole story about Andrew Quincy smelled like . . . like yesterday's black pudding. And he flat out lied about being at White's. He doesn't even know the steward's name, yet he claims to have interviewed him personally."

"Then we need to check out Quincy," said Anya. "We need to find out who he really is."

"Agreed."

"Should we ask at White's?"

"No, Graham was right about one thing. If Quincy is affiliated with the club in some kind of security role, I doubt they'll tell us anything about him. I have a better idea. Let's check him out ourselves."

"How?"

"By following him."

"But he is following us."

"Exactly. So he shouldn't be too hard to find. Come on. Time's a wasting."

The agents walked down the Strand, past coffee shops and bookstores and taverns, cabs and London's ubiquitous red, double-decker buses passing them on the street. They walked slowly, knowing that Quincy, whoever he was, was probably behind them somewhere and they wanted to give him plenty of opportunity to keep his sights on them. Each agent carried a small gym duffel. Eventually, they came upon Charing Cross train station and went inside. They walked halfway through the expansive station and stopped. Then they turned to each other and embraced warmly, taking their time to make sure Quincy could see them through the crowd. Their ersatz goodbyes said, they set off in opposite directions, each walking toward one of the six rail platforms of Charing Cross.

At a ticket machine, Anya slowly turned around and, through the mass of people around her all traipsing toward their respective platforms to board their respective trains, saw nobody resembling Quincy in her general vicinity. She walked back toward where she'd embraced Kori and soon spotted her fellow Rampart agent in a far ticket line. Ten paces behind her, looking as casual and unassuming as he could, was Quincy.

Anya pulled out her phone. *He picked you*, she texted.

Kori glanced down at her phone, bought a ticket, and then strode into a women's restroom adjacent to the ticket machines. Anya watched as Quincy took a position across from the restroom, leaning against the wall under a clock. Women came and went from the restroom, including, eventually, a blond woman in a white, hooded sweatshirt and dark red sneakers. Clutching a Harrod's bag, she left the restroom and walked unnoticed by Quincy through the crowd and to the other end of the station where Anya was waiting for her.

"You look good as a blonde," Anya said.

"Oh, yeah?" said Kori. "And what about the rest of the ensemble?"

"The ugly sneakers have to go."

"Aw, really?"

"Yes. Even you cannot make them work."

"I guess. So what's our man doing?"

"He's still waiting."

"How long you figure he'll stand there?"

"Who can say?"

The answer came eight minutes later. From across the station, the agents could see Quincy stepping toward the restroom. He glanced about the immediate area before hesitating and then, mind made up, he darted inside. Fifteen seconds later, he popped back out with at least one woman giving him a dirty look. He raised his head and scanned the area as Kori and Anya turned their backs, Kori shielding her undisguised partner. When they looked around a moment later, Quincy was heading quickly toward the exit, talking into his phone.

"He's on the move," Kori said. "The predator has now become the prey. Let's go."

They walked toward the exit, careful to remain unseen. Out front, they watched as a dark sedan pulled up. Quincy got into the passenger side and the car pulled away. Kori flagged down a cab and the agents slid in.

"Follow that car!" Kori barked to the driver, pointing ahead. Then, turning to Anya and laughing, she said, "I've always wanted to jump into a cab and say that. Can you believe in all of my years of agency work, I've never done so?"

"Another milestone," said Anya. "A classic spy cliché."

"Indeed. But, driver, seriously. We need you to follow that car. If you'd be so kind."

# 12

— • —

The dark sedan traveled east, more or less following the Thames along its north side.

The cabbie was the talkative type. "Where you ladies from?" he asked.

"The US," Kori replied.

"Well, hope you're enjoying your stay, yeah? So who's in the car we're following?"

"Oh, just some friends."

"Uh-huh. So how about our missing prince, huh? Crazy, innit? Know what I think? I think it's all bollocks, that's why I think."

"Is that right?"

"Sure. Publicity stunt, if you ask me. You barely ever hear of the bloke. He's the 'reclusive prince,' yeah? All you hear about are Charles and Andrew and Edward. And sometimes Anne. Blimey, you hear more about the grandchildren. It's always William this and Harry that, yeah? So I'm thinkin' maybe old Grayson wants a little of the limelight for hisself. He staged the whole bloody thing is what I'm sayin'. That's my theory."

"Interesting. Well, maybe you're right."

"Aye, you know I am. Staged the whole bloody thing," he repeated.

Along their route, as they drove farther and farther from Central London, Kori noticed the neighborhoods becoming more and more sketchy. Clean office towers and apartments gradually made way for more industrialized sections that ultimately led to seedier streets and vacant buildings.

"What area is this?" Kori asked the cabbie.

"Borough of Rothton, ma'am," he replied. "I'm afraid it's not a very nice area. Mostly low-end housing, you know, with some old factories and dockyards and such. Lots of crime and drugs and the like, yeah? Gets a bit rough in spots, I will say. Are you sure you want me to keep followin'?"

"Absolutely. But not too close."

"And you say these blokes ahead of us are friends of yours?"

"Sure."

"Okay, ma'am."

With the driver keeping a distance of about fifty yards, the agents eventually saw the sedan turning south toward the Thames. Three blocks later, past a few unkempt red brick industrial buildings and one sleazy-looking pub, the car turned into the parking lot of a warehouse that rested on the river.

"Pull over here," Kori said, well before the parking lot. "Come on, Anya."

"Begging your pardon, ladies, but are you sure you want to get out here? I don't know what your aim is or who your friends are, and maybe it's not for me to say, but it's not exactly the safest place to be, yeah? I'm not a hundred percent comfortable here myself, I must say."

"We will be fine," Anya said handing the driver the fare. "Thanks for the ride."

"Should I wait for you?"

"That won't be necessary, thank you."

The driver shrugged, took the money, and pulled a U-turn. Kori, who had since ditched the wig, replaced the red sneakers with her black leather ankle boots, and stuffed the Harrod's bag into her gym duffle, suggested to Anya that they drop the duffels where they were. "We can hide them in those weeds over there," she said, "behind the utility pole."

They started slowly walking down the road the sedan had driven moments before, past the unkempt red brick buildings and the sleazy-looking pub, a dank place in a small, single-story frame building called Louie's, although the "u" and the "i" in the eponymous neon sign were both burned out. The door was slightly ajar and, as they walked past, the agents could see a long bar, bathed mostly in darkness, with a couple of weary-looking patrons leaning up against it over their glasses.

"Fancy a pint?" Kori said.

"Maybe later," Anya said, wrinkling her nose.

"Yes, much later," Kori agreed.

Soon they were upon the warehouse and could see the sedan in the parking lot with a couple of other cars, the occupants presumably inside the building. On the back side of the building was the brown Thames, and through the industrial buildings that lined the river bank, they could see a barge floating by. They hung back behind a chain-link fence that was covered in overgrown ivy. The metal warehouse had a small brick office building at the front with a sign by the door that read "Hudson Imports."

"What would a White's security person be doing in there?" Kori asked.

"Maybe it's his day job," Anya offered.

"Hmm . . . maybe. Well, let's find out, shall we?"

The agents steered clear of the front office, sprinting from the fence to the side of the warehouse and then peering around the back where the building abutted a long concrete dock. A sixty-foot trawler was moored at the dock and a man on the deck was turning the winch of a jib crane that had been swung over the dock, lowering a pallet of boxes. Another man on the dock was standing beneath and just to the side of the pallet, guiding it down to the ground where a third man was waiting with a pallet mover. Kori noticed a speedboat tied up behind the trawler, an incongruous sight on this industrial section of the river Thames.

"Easy does it," the man guiding the load called to the winch operator on the boat deck.

Anya and Kori crouched down and watched from behind the corner of the building as the man with the pallet mover eventually rolled the load through the rear roll-up door of the warehouse.

"One more," the man on the ship called down and he set about hooking the crane's hoist onto another bundle of boxes. Soon, the man with the pallet mover came back out.

"Here's our chance," Kori whispered. Anya nodded. With the three men engaged with the lowering of the second bundle, Kori and Anya stayed low and crept swiftly along the back of the building, Kori in front. She hesitated at the door for a moment to take a quick glance inside, and then entered the warehouse and ducked to the side, Anya right behind her.

The two agents kneeled behind a wide stack of boxes and took in their surroundings. The small warehouse was cramped with rows of pallets of boxes and cartons. Nobody else was in the warehouse, but across the floor, Kori could see a door that led into the front offices. She pointed toward it. "That's where Quincy must be," she whispered.

"Then we need to sneak in there somehow," Anya whispered back.

Kori was ready to reply when the office door swung open and none other than Quincy himself walked into the warehouse carrying a small canvas bag under his arm. The agents made themselves even lower to the ground and Kori peeked around the stack of boxes to see Quincy meet up with the man with the pallet mover as he rolled the second pallet into the warehouse.

"This is it, boss," the man reported.

Behind him came the other man from the dock, plus the man who'd been up on the deck of the trawler. Finally, following them all into the warehouse was someone Kori and Anya hadn't noticed on the ship. He wore a gray baseball cap and strode with purpose, approaching Quincy and extending his hand.

"Always good to see you, mate," he smiled as Quincy shook his hand.

"And you," Quincy replied. "And that bloody fine boat of yours."

"Didn't expect to see you here, Quince. Thought you were on that other project."

"Yeah, well, I took a detour. Thought I'd give the other project a rest. Besides, I wouldn't miss the chance to be here for another one of your special deliveries."

The captain of the trawler nodded. "Sure, sure. Well, you'll find all the merchandise you asked for here. Just like always."

"No doubt. You're a good bloke, Cooksey. And you'll find everything you've asked for right here." Quincy handed over the canvas bag. "Just like always. You can count it if you'd like."

"No need, Quince. You're a good bloke yourself. Call me when you're ready for more."

"Aye, you can count on it. The boss has been happy so far."

"Good to hear. There's plenty more where this came from. Well, cheers, mate." The captain shook Quincy's hand again and turned and walked out of the warehouse, his crewmate in tow.

"Okay, fellows," Quincy said to his own men. "That's it for today. Leave the stuff here and close up."

"Say," one of the men said, lowering the roll-up door, "why *are* you here, Quincy? Thought you were following around that American bird you'd talked about."

"Never you mind, Fisher. I'm takin' a break, okay? I know just where the American is." Kori looked at Anya and grinned. "Figured I needed to come back here and make sure you boys are doin' your jobs. Good help is hard to find these days. Now, go into the office and collect your pay from McCarthy and then beat it. We'll call you when we need you again."

The men did as Quincy said while Quincy opened one of the newly acquired boxes and nodded approvingly. Then he set it down and walked back into the office himself, turning out the overhead lights behind him and leaving the warehouse in darkness.

Kori and Anya stood, turned on the flashlights of their phones, and looked about. Kori walked over to the box Quincy had opened and opened it herself.

"Well, that's a surprise," she whispered. Anya came over to see the contents.

"What did you expect?" she asked.

"I don't know. Drugs, I guess. You know, baggies full of white powder or something. Certainly not these."

Anya and Kori each lifted out a purse with the unmistakable double "G" logo of Gucci. Anya opened a second carton and pulled out a Gucci wallet. In other boxes, there were hats and gloves and scarves.

"Gucci merchandise," Kori said.

"Hardly," said Anya. "Knock-offs. Probably made in China and smuggled in on Chinese container ships.

That trawler was not an ocean-going rig. They probably picked up the shipment in some other English port, like Southampton, to bring here."

"With the idea of getting it out on the streets of London and selling it as genuine."

"Right."

"Well, this certainly raises more questions than it answers. Come on, let's get out of here."

"It seems as if we are locked in."

"There," said Kori, pointing to a side door. "I could pick that lock with my hands tied behind my back."

"After you."

As they turned, the office door suddenly opened and the overhead lights came on. The man Quincy called Fisher had left his car keys on the shipping desk and was standing in the doorway with Kori in plain sight. Anya was still hidden. The man took a few steps into the warehouse, the self-closing office door swinging shut behind him. He turned as if to yell something toward the office, but Kori had drawn her Glock and was pointing it directly at him.

"Nuh-uh," she said. "Not a word."

The man raised his hands. "What do you want?"

"Who do you work for?" Kori replied.

"Me? His name is Quincy."

"And who does Quincy work for?"

"Don't know, ma'am. Never met him. I'm just a temp, you see. Paid to come in and help with the occasional unloading of a shipment. I just met Quincy two weeks ago. Who are you, anyway? Am I in some kind of trouble?"

Kori sensed the man was telling the truth. Anya sensed it, too. There was nothing more to be gained by questioning him and everything to lose. At any moment, Quincy could come back into the warehouse. Which is why Anya, having slipped unseen around a row of boxes, had come up unnoticed behind the man. It was time to end the conversation.

Kori held the man's eyes and said, "Down on your knees, mate."

The man kneeled. From behind, Anya quickly wrapped her right arm around his neck, her elbow under his chin. Then she slid her left hand behind his head and locked her arms. The move was so quick that the man didn't have time to resist. Anya squeezed hard on the side of the man's neck, temporarily cutting off the blood supply to his brain. He was out cold in seconds. Anya held the position for the perfect amount of time to ensure no permanent damage would be done, but that the man would be unconscious for the time Kori needed to pick the lock.

Anya laid the man on the floor. "Go!" she said, jumping up and heading toward the door. Kori was already there. With her lockpick tools, she jiggled the lock for a moment and in no time, the door was open and the agents were outside.

"Classic sleeper hold," Kori said as the two jogged up the street past the pub to retrieve their duffels. "And expertly performed, I have to say."

"Thanks," Anya said. "It is a favorite of mine. Dangerous if not done properly, however."

"I'm sure. Where'd you learn it?"

"My father taught me. It was a popular maneuver on the professional wrestling shows we used to watch when I was little."

"Marx Brothers, the Three Stooges, professional wrestling . . . my, is there no end to the amount of high-class culture you were exposed to?"

"What can I say?" Anya grinned. "I was a lucky girl."

**13**

—·—

In Mayfair Village, a fifteen-minute cab ride west of the Savoy, rests the venerable Connaught, a supremely elegant hotel dating back to 1815. It was called the Prince of Saxe Coburg Hotel when it first opened in the form of twin Georgian houses. Those were torn down in 1892, and the hotel was reopened in 1897 as the Coburg. But, with World War I raging, the Coburg was renamed in 1917 to something less German sounding, though a bar within—the Coburg Bar—still paid homage. The Connaught was named in honor of Queen Victoria's third son, the Duke of Connaught. Like the Savoy, the hotel has been the home of celebrities and royalty alike. French president Charles de Gaulle resided there for a time during World War II, meeting American general Dwight D. Eisenhower not far away to plan the D-day invasion.

Now, having checked out of the Savoy and made the Connaught their new home for the foreseeable future, Kori Briggs and Anya Kovalev were enjoying a drink at the Coburg and splitting a club sandwich. They knew where

Andrew Quincy was but Quincy didn't know where they were.

"Just as it should be," Kori was saying to Anya.

"Yes, but we are still in the dark about *who* Quincy is," Anya remarked.

"Let's find out," Kori said, reaching for her phone. In a moment, she had Agent Darren Cooper on the line. "Coop, see what you can uncover on a London business in the borough of Rothton called Hudson Imports. It's on a street called Glendover, right on the river."

"Sure," came Cooper's reply. "Why?"

"Well, a guy who's been following me, a guy Victor Graham was certain worked security at White's, just happens to be employed there in the business of importing counterfeit goods. Fake Gucci merchandise to be exact."

"Strange."

"Stranger still, the guy's supposedly a friend of our fair prince. In fact, he paid visits to his home twice before the kidnapping. So while you're looking up Hudson Imports, check out the name Andrew Quincy, would ya? That's the guy in question."

"Will do, Kori. I'll get back as soon as I find something."

Kori hung up and turned to Anya. "So why do you think Agent Graham lied about Quincy?"

"It is obvious," Anya said. "He is embarrassed that he did not know about him, so he made something up."

"You think?"

"Yes. You presented him with information he did not have but should have had. Your investigation turned up something his did not. He could not very well admit that you had one-upped him, so he pretended that he knew about Quincy."

"So . . . ego, you're saying?"

"Ego."

"Hmm . . . I suppose you're right."

"But there is a bigger question, Kori."

"Which is?"

"Why is a guy like Quincy involved with an English prince in the first place?"

"Right. Why is Prince Grayson slumming around with the dregs from a smuggling operation in one of the worst parts of town?"

"Meanwhile, there is still the matter of the whereabouts of Spenser Burke and Newton Dempsey. Let us not forget them."

"I know. Lots of loose ends, Anya. Maybe another drink would help."

"Couldn't hurt."

Over a second round, the agents pondered the situation as far as they could and then chatted about personal matters, Anya eventually asking about Kori's mom. "Oh, she's fine," Kori said. "She thinks I'm in Boston with Gladstone Conveyor on a big installation. You know what's funny? She's crazy about the royal family. Always has been. Reads every tabloid article she can get her hands on."

"The royal family seems to resonate with people all over the world," said Anya. "Not just in the UK."

"My mom's living proof of that. Imagine if she knew I was investigating the kidnapping of Prince Grayson."

"She would be very proud."

"Yes," Kori said wistfully. "Yes, I suppose she would be."

Finally, Kori's phone rang.

"Kori, I think I've got what you need," Cooper said.

"Lay it on me, Coop."

"Turns out that Hudson Imports is on a very long list of companies that are believed, as yet unproven, to be owned by the Turner crime family."

"Turner?"

"*The* London mafia, Kori. The Turner family is the biggest crime syndicate in the UK. They're into a little bit of everything. Gambling, drugs, loan sharking, prostitution, even human trafficking. And, yes, the sale of counterfeit goods."

"So law enforcement knows about Hudson Imports?"

"Sure they do."

"So why are they still in business? Why haven't they been shut down, the people arrested?"

"You want the disappointing answer or the *really* disappointing answer?"

"Let's start with the first and work up to the second."

"These mob guys are simply very good at what they do. They always stay a step ahead of the cops. They move their businesses around and change the names all the time. Sure, Hudson Imports is on the radar but in a month, it's probably going to be somewhere else and in a different location. By the time police get a warrant on a place, it's typically too late. And then there's the question of proving guilt. The mob has money. They get the best lawyers. Hell, they've got lawyers on their payroll. Full-time guys."

"I see what you mean."

"And of course it's difficult to find these businesses in the first place because, well, nobody ever talks. Speaking out about the London mafia isn't the healthiest activity to engage in. It's impossible to get witnesses to testify against them."

"So what's the *really* disappointing answer? Wait, don't tell me; let me guess. Payoffs to the cops."

"Bingo. Cops, magistrates, judges, assembly members—the mob's got a lot of people in their pocket. And of course, the head guys keep themselves so far above the day-to-day goings-on that nobody can touch them. It's an unbelievably sophisticated organization, rivaling the best crime syndicates in the world."

"Lovely. So what about Andrew Quincy? Did you find anything on him?"

"Yes, it seems that Andrew Augustin Quincy is a low-level lieutenant. Took a while to find him, but, fortunately, there's a lot of intelligence on the London mafia and after cross-checking several law enforcement databases, I was able to locate him. Apparently, he started out with them several years ago as nothing more than muscle. You know, a hired goon. Seems he's working his way up."

"So it would seem. He's now running a counterfeit merchandise operation."

"Right. And apparently reporting directly to the leader himself."

"Doesn't seem so low-level. Did he ever work at White's?"

"Nope. Never."

"I'm not surprised. Okay, thanks, Coop. I'll be in touch."

"Be careful, Kori. These mob guys don't play around. And for whatever reason, they've personally entrusted this Quincy guy to keep tabs on you. You're in the crosshairs of one of the most dangerous organizations on the planet."

"So what now?" Anya asked.

"I'm not sure," Kori replied. "Things just got more complicated, didn't they? Andrew Quincy, who never worked at White's—in direct contradiction to MI5 agent Victor Graham's assertion—is a member of the UK's biggest crime family. He's also somehow acquainted with Prince Grayson, who received him in his home twice in the days leading up to his kidnapping. So does this mean the London mafia is behind the kidnapping?"

"That is not exactly the modus operandi of the mob," Anya said. "They are into the usual illegal activities, running them out of businesses that appear legitimate to launder their money. They continue to exist because they are smart enough to keep to what they know. Why engage in something like the kidnapping of a royal prince? Why something so high profile? It makes no sense."

"Agreed. It would be way too big a risk. Something like this could bring down their entire organization. So do you think that maybe Quincy is operating on his own?"

"That would be the more likely scenario. If he is involved at all, that is. The connection is—how do you say?—tenuous, Kori. Okay, he visited with Grayson a couple of times. But when you stop and think about it, that is all we know. And so far as we can tell, he is not connected with Dempsey or Burke at all. Let us not forget the two main players in the prince's kidnapping."

"True. Neither Burke nor Dempsey has any ties to the mafia, so far as we know. I mean, I suppose it's possible that maybe Burke does. But Dempsey? How would he even know anybody with the London mob?"

"Right."

"So, it's just coincidence that Quincy knows Grayson?"

"Apparently. And consider this, Kori. Even on his own, Quincy would not be involved in a kidnapping. Why would *he* risk it? He has a good position with the mob, right? He reports directly to the Turners. He is moving up the ladder."

"True. And he wouldn't dare expose the mob. If it came out that he was involved with the kidnapping, the Turner crime family would be dragged into the middle of it."

"Yes."

"So it's a complete coincidence?"

"It has to be."

"So why is he following us, Anya? We still don't have an answer to that. Why is someone from the London mafia following us around London?"

"Perhaps he is just your ordinary stalker," Anya grinned. "With a crush on you."

"Ha! That's all I need. A crush from a mobster."

"But in all seriousness, there is more to it than why he is following us, Kori. Another big question presents itself: How does he know who we are?"

"Or who does he *think* we are?"

"Right."

"I think I'm getting a headache."

Kori's phone rang. She picked it up and looked at the screen. "Wow," she said, "this is a surprise."

"Who is it?"

"Victor Graham, of all people." Then she answered. "Agent Graham, to what do I owe the pleasure?"

"Agent Briggs, I just thought you should be made aware of an update to the case."

"Oh? *Moi?* You're including *me* in on your updates? I must say I'm flattered."

"Yes, well you see, it involves the one single lead you were able to provide us. Unfortunately, that lead was a dead end. And I must say, it's a shame. We've been spending precious man-hours on it. Man-hours that could have been spent in more productive ways. All for naught, I'm afraid."

"My lead? You mean the name Spenser Burke?"

"Precisely."

"Wait, are you telling me that he's not involved? Because I'd find that very hard to believe, Graham."

"Believe it, Agent Briggs. You can go back to America now. Your Spenser Burke fellow has been unequivocally cleared of any involvement with the prince's kidnapping."

"How can you be so sure?"

"Because we've found him, you see. And I dare say he's worse than not involved."

"What do you mean? Where did you find him?"

"In the Thames, I'm afraid. He was found floating in the river. Spenser Burke can't be involved in the kidnapping because, you see, Agent Briggs,  Spenser Burke is as dead as dead can be."

# 14

—•—

"I'm telling you, dear, it's all over the news," Joan Briggs said. "It's all the networks are covering."

"Serves me right for not paying attention to current events," Kori told her mom. She and Anya had essentially quit for the day, agreeing to meet for breakfast the next morning to reset. They'd finished their drinks, eaten some dessert, and realized they were unmistakably frustrated and unequivocally stumped. They agreed a good night's sleep couldn't hurt, and Kori had decided to call her mother before slipping into a hot tub.

"The whole world is wondering where the prince is," her mother continued. "I mean, it's as if he simply disappeared. Just fell off the face of the planet!"

"Crazy, huh? Well, I'm sure he'll turn up. Maybe he's just on some private vacation somewhere."

"Without telling anyone about it?"

"Well, he's a prince. Probably figured he didn't need to."

"I'm not so sure, Kori. You know what I read in *Star Globe Magazine*?"

"Oh boy, is that one of your gossip tabloids, Mom?"

"Kori, *Star Globe Magazine* is a well-respected news source! They were the ones who broke the George Clooney story, remember?"

"Who could forget?"

"Anyway, they're reporting that Prince Grayson has a serious gambling problem."

"Really?"

"Really. He's a gambling addict. It's been hidden all these years, but apparently, it's caught up with him. He owes a *ton* of money."

"To whom?"

"Well, the article doesn't exactly say."

"Then how does *Star Globe* know he owes a ton of money?"

"They *know*, Kori. It's their job to know. They're investigative reporters, remember? They investigate."

Kori winced.

Joan continued. "Anyway, they're thinking he couldn't pay off his gambling debts and so someone came along and pulled a Jimmy Hoffa on him. Maybe this guy whose picture they keep showing. They're thinking the prince's body might never be found. Isn't that something? The whole thing gives me shivers."

Kori was thoughtful for a moment then said, "Mom, where is this *Star Globe* article? Can I find it online?"

"Sure. That's where I read it. It's on their website. Of course, I subscribe so I get notifications. I'll send you a link if you'd like."

"Would you, Mom? Sounds kind of interesting. Maybe I should start paying more attention to what's going on in the world, huh?"

"You should, Kori! You get too wrapped up in your job. By the way, how's everything going there in Boston?"

"It's fine, Mom. You know, same old stuff. Work's work. Speaking of which, I better get back to it. My coffee break is just about over and I've got a lot to do yet today. Send me that link, though, will you?"

"I will, dear. Don't work too hard."

"I'll try not to. Love you, Mom."

A few minutes later, Kori was reading a story entitled Prince Grayson's Gambling Addiction Might Have Cost Him His Life! Ten minutes after that, she was mulling the story over from the comfort of her hot bath, weighing the credibility of *Star Globe Magazine*, and trying to find a way to make the story fit into the reality of the missing prince.

"*Star Globe Magazine*, Kori?"

"I know, I know, but keep an open mind for a second." At Jean-Georges restaurant at the Connaught, the agents were having the Connaught Breakfast. Kori was halfway through an apple chausson while Anya was working on her scrambled eggs.

Just three days remained until Dempsey's deadline.

"Anya, Grayson's valet, Kingsley Moore, confided to me that Grayson and Sir John Holland play cards at White's all the time and for pretty high stakes."

"So? They are both rich men."

"Of course. But did you know that John Holland's middle name is Emery?"

"No. So what?"

"JEH, Anya. Sir John Holland is the founder and president of JEH Financial Group."

Anya put her fork down. "Interesting, my friend. I did not know that little piece of information."

"Neither did I until I did a quick search. I suppose I should have, but it really never occurred to me to make the connection. I had no idea how Holland made his money. But think about it. Those promissory notes. There was nothing in them about the nature of the money owed. Could they be for gambling debts that Grayson owes Holland?"

"Maybe. But why run the debts through his company, Kori? Why not a personal loan? And why put it in writing at all if they are such good friends?"

"I don't know. But there must be a reason."

"Maybe they are not such good friends."

"Maybe not."

"But, Kori, you are assuming there is truth to the *Star Globe* story."

"Yeah, I know. That's definitely the weakest link of the theory."

"Was there a byline? We could question the reporter. Determine his source."

"Yeah, I thought of that. The reporter was some guy by the name of Cameron Riley. One of their top reporters, from what I could gather. The problem is, talking to him would only give him more fodder for his next piece. Can't you see the headline? 'American Investigators Now on the Hunt for the Prince.'"

"True."

"If you want to keep a low profile, you don't go to *Star Globe Magazine*. My guess is that this guy Riley's source, if there's any truth to the story, is someone at White's. That's where the card games took place, after all. Maybe even Edwards, the steward we met at the door. I know how these rags work. They offer a ton of money to someone who can give them a scoop. Everyone's got their price."

"Or maybe it was Kingsley Moore. As his valet, he probably knows as much about Grayson's personal life as anyone. And he was the one who mentioned the card games."

"Well, yeah, maybe."

"Was there any mention in the article of John Holland?"

"None."

"Holland's name is a pretty relevant piece of the story. If it's true."

"Right. So whoever spilled the beans about the debts must have kept Holland's name out of it."

"Then that would suggest Edwards."

"Why?"

"He is the steward," Anya said. "He may have his price for information, but he is still sworn to protect the privacy of the club's members."

"He sure wasn't in any hurry to tell us anything."

"So presumably he was willing to talk about the gambling debts, but stopped short of giving the *Star Globe* reporter the name of Holland."

"Yes, I suppose you're right. But you know what? It doesn't really matter. It doesn't even matter if the article wasn't entirely factual. We have Kingsley Moore's confirmation of high-stakes poker games between Grayson and Holland, and we have confirmation of large amounts of money owed to JEH Financial, Holland's company. My mother's interest in the tabloids, God bless her, connected the dots for us."

"Ah, but here is what we do not have, Kori: A connection between those things and the fact that the prince has been kidnapped by Newton Dempsey of Boston, Massachusetts."

Kori was quiet for a moment. "You're right, of course, Anya," she said at last. "Damn. So you think this is another rabbit hole like the Spenser Burke lead or following Andrew Quincy around?"

"Well ... maybe. Sir John Holland certainly doesn't need to be involved in the kidnapping of a prince any more than the Turner crime family does. If one were looking for likely suspects, those two would be pretty far toward the bottom of the list."

"Damn," Kori repeated.

"And so we are stuck, it seems."

"Maybe. But, rabbit hole or no rabbit hole, I think we ought to follow up on this matter of Grayson's debts, don't you?"

"How?"

"I think we need to confront Parker Bates with what we now know. He was the guy holding the promissory notes, after all. Heck, maybe he was the guy who spilled the beans to Cameron Riley. Why did he keep Grayson's debts from me when I questioned him? What is he hiding?"

"A legitimate question."

"Let's make Bates's townhouse today's first stop."

"I have no better ideas, my friend. Down the rabbit hole we go."

"You again," Bates said answering his door. "And now I see you've brought a friend. Have you any news on the prince?"

"I'm afraid we still have more questions than answers," said Kori. "More questions than what I had the other day, as a matter of fact, Mr. Bates."

"Well, Ms. Briggs, I have told you everything I know, I assure you. Now, if you'll excuse me . . ." Bates began to close the door.

"How come you didn't tell me about the 632,980 pounds?" Kori said, sliding her foot into the doorway.

Bates looked taken aback for a moment but recovered quickly. "I'm sure I don't know what you mean."

"Sure you do. The 632,980 pounds that the prince owes to JEH Financial. John Emery Holland."

Bates's expression turned into one of resignation. He opened the door and waved the agents inside. "How did you find out?" he asked.

"It doesn't matter," Kori replied as the three moved into the living room. "The important thing is we believe that's a pretty relevant nugget of information, wouldn't you agree?"

"I'm afraid I would not agree, Ms. Briggs. I cannot see how it is the least bit relevant to my employer's disappearance."

"When you owe somebody a lot of money and you can't pay, sometimes strange things happen, Mr. Bates. Dangerous things, at that."

"Are you suggesting John Holland is behind the kidnapping? That's preposterous. If I thought that, believe me, I would have said something to you. Don't you think I'd like for Prince Grayson to be found? To be brought safely home? He is my boss but he is also my friend, Ms. Briggs. I didn't mention the debt because, well, first of all, you didn't ask."

"I asked you about Grayson's relationship with Holland."

"Second of all, can you imagine the embarrassment if the prince's debt became a matter of public record? It's bad enough that the gossip rags are reporting a gambling addiction. It's sickening."

Kori and Anya exchanged glances, both thinking the same thing: It must not have been Bates who spilled the beans.

"Does the prince *have* a gambling addiction?" Kori asked.

"Certainly not, Ms. Briggs. Well, I mean, the prince likes to wager, of course. But it's all in fun. He does like his card games, I must say. And the horses. Sometimes he bets on football. And rugby. But a gambling addiction?"

"I don't know, Bates. You don't get that far into debt by having total control over your actions. Most people would have stopped long before."

"Maybe," Bates acknowledged. "Nevertheless, Ms. Briggs, my interest, and my job as the prince's private secretary is to make certain that information such as this does not come to light. Surely, you can understand that."

Kori looked at Anya who shrugged.

"Okay, Mr. Bates," Kori said. "We understand. The prince's secret is safe with us."

"Thank you."

"So who do you think tipped off the tabloids? *Star Globe* was the first to break the story of his gambling."

"I assume it was a lucky guess on their part. They make stuff up. Every now and again, they're bound to get close to the truth, but it's typically an accident."

"Well, listen, Mr. Bates, as long as we're here, if you have any other little details we should know about, this would be a good time to clue us in."

"I can assure you that you now know everything I know."

The agents walked toward the door. Bates opened it and then turned to Kori with a somber expression. "You will find him, won't you Ms. Briggs?"

"We'll give it everything we can, Mr. Bates."

Bates closed the door behind them. On the sidewalk, Kori turned to Anya. "What do you think?"

"He does not know anything else. You saw that look on his face. By not telling you about the debt or the supposed gambling problem, he was only trying to be a good employee."

"I suppose you're right."

"He is a sincere man. In a tough spot."

"Agreed."

"So what now?"

"Hmm . . ." Kori contemplated the situation for a moment and then replied, "I'd love to talk to John Holland, wouldn't you? I agree with Bates that his involvement would be 'preposterous,' but he's got to know *something*."

"What makes you think so?"

"Because billionaires always know something. That's how they get to be billionaires. They have their fingers on the pulse of the world around them, and for Holland, that includes the world of Prince Grayson. The only thing is, we could never get near him. Guys like Holland keep themselves completely inaccessible. His assistant would refer us to his executive assistant who would refer us to his secretary who would refer us to his executive secretary who would refer us to his personal, private, executive secretary who would probably refer us to his attorney. We'd need a warrant just to get in the front door."

"Yes, I see what you mean."

"But that doesn't mean we can't follow him around for a bit. Maybe corner him somewhere and start asking him some questions."

"Okay, I'm game. Where do we start?"

"Well, we know where JEH Financial Group is located. Let's start there."

As Kori knew all too well, the life of an intelligence agent isn't all nonstop action and adventure. Sometimes, many times, in fact, it includes mind-numbing surveillance for hours on end. And so it was that she found herself sitting on a bench across from a five-story glass and concrete building at 23 Queen Victoria Street, the headquarters for JEH Financial Group.

And sitting. And sitting.

Anya was watching the back entrance of the building. The pair had rented a car which, for lack of parking on London's streets, was double-parked within Anya's view, allowing her to jump up and drive it around the block anytime she noticed parking enforcement nearby, which, fortunately, wasn't very often.

James Foster at Rampart HQ had texted both agents several pictures of Sir John Holland so they had a good idea of whom they were looking for. There were precious few pictures that could be found online; Holland kept himself out of the spotlight. Nobody seemed to know very much about his personal life. If Grayson was the reclusive prince, Holland was the reclusive billionaire. All that was generally known about Sir John Holland was that he was one of the richest men in the United Kingdom.

For four hours the agents waited. Finally, Kori noticed a black Rolls-Royce Phantom pull up to the main entrance of the building. A neatly dressed driver got out and walked around to the passenger side, positioned to open the rear door for whomever the car was meant for. Kori called Anya on her cell.

"Anya, bring the car around!" she said. "A five-hundred-thousand-dollar, chauffeur-driven automobile just pulled up. Who do you think the passenger is going to be?"

"On my way," Anya replied.

Kori saw their Hyundai come around the block just about the same time that none other than Sir John Holland himself came out of the front door. Fifty-five years old, Holland was tall with a light mustache and his gait was purposeful; he carried himself almost regally, Kori observed, like you'd expect of a billionaire. Holland slid into the back seat of the Rolls just as Anya pulled over, half a block behind. Kori trotted back to the rental and got in. The driver of the Rolls pulled away. The Hyundai followed.

The route took them east for fifteen minutes to the A13, through Whitechapel for another fifteen minutes, and then on a side street.

"Kori, I cannot get used to this driving on the left," said Anya. "How do they do it here?"

"You're doing fine," Kori said.

The Rolls took a right from the side street and soon stopped in front of a small, two-story, brick office building. Anya drove past and then pulled over a block ahead in front of an apartment building. Both agents turned and watched through the rear window as Holland exited the Rolls and got into the driver's seat of a much more modest car.

"Cripes, Anya, it's an everyday Volvo," said Kori. "Why is one of the richest men in the country driving a Volvo?"

"Why is he driving at all?" said Anya. "He has a driver. With a Rolls. Why the switch?"

"Guess we'll find out. Here he comes." The two agents scrunched down in their seats as the Volvo drove past. Then Anya put the Hyundai in drive and the pursuit continued. The Volvo drove slowly, forcing Anya to drive much slower than she was accustomed to. She repeatedly had to lay off the gas to keep a decent distance between her and Holland. A few times, Holland got a green traffic light and Anya arrived at the intersection after the light had turned red. But she didn't allow a red light to stop her for long. As soon as the traffic cleared, she'd forge ahead.

"I hope we don't get pulled over," Kori said after one such excursion through a red light.

"I will plead ignorance," Anya said. "Red lights, green lights, driving on the left—who can keep track of it all?"

The cars meandered for several miles until, finally, the agents found themselves driving down familiar streets.

"Rothton!" Kori said.

"One and the same," Anya nodded. "What is our man doing here, of all places?"

They watched as the Volvo took a turn toward the river Thames, past unkempt red brick buildings. Soon it stopped in front of a sleazy-looking pub that the agents recognized immediately.

"I'll be damned," Kori said.

The Volvo parked and Sir John Holland, dressed in a suit that was probably worth more than the pub itself, strolled into the dank joint, past the sign out front, with the darkened "u" and "i," that announced "Louie's."

# 15

— · —

Anya parked down the street and the agents walked up to the back of Louie's. Just below the roofline of the single-story building, a small rear window about nine feet from the ground with a single jalousie sash was cranked open. "Probably to let the dank out," Kori surmised.

"They would need more than that," Anya remarked.

"Like a tornado. Anyway, we don't dare walk around the front and try to look in through the door. You want to try the window?"

"Sure. Give me a boost."

Anya pressed her foot into Kori's cupped hands and drew herself up to the level of the window. She peered in and gazed about the bar below. Four people. The bartender, a customer standing at the end of the bar nursing a dark beer, and, centered at the bar, Sir John Holland in an animated conversation with none other than Andrew Quincy.

"That's right, Coop. Anything and everything you can find on Sir John Holland. We'll be waiting."

The agents were back at the Connaught hanging out in Anya's room and planning their next move. Anya had seen the conversation between Holland and Quincy but could hear nothing from the small rear window. Ten minutes after Holland had made his way into the pub, he'd left. He hadn't even stayed long enough to have a drink. The agents followed him back to the office building where he parked his Volvo and watched as he got into the waiting Rolls. Then he was driven back to the headquarters of JEH Financial.

"Cooper's going to forward me a full report," Kori said, hanging up the phone.

"What are we hoping to find, my friend?"

"Who knows? A connection, I guess. A connection between one of the wealthiest men in the UK and the Turner crime family."

"Kori, that connection might go no further than Quincy. We still do not know that Quincy is not acting on his own."

"Either way, why is Holland dealing with a guy who's connected in the first place? Holland, a friend of the prince, no less. Oh, there's my phone. Looks like it's the chief." She answered. "Chief, I was just talking to Cooper. We're going to—"

"Agent Briggs," Eaglethorpe began, "I'm aware that you were talking to Agent Cooper. I'd like to know why."

Kori had worked with Rampart director Richard Eaglethorpe long enough to understand his moods. The tone of his voice indicated that he was not in a good one. "Well, Chief," she replied, "we're following up on John Holland. I don't know if Coop explained, but Holland is apparently working with an integral member of the Turner crime family."

"Yes, Agent Cooper explained. What he didn't explain is what Holland has to do with the kidnapping of Prince Grayson."

"Well, Holland and Grayson are close friends. Besties, you could say."

"Yes? And?"

"And the Turner guy—Quincy—was seen with Grayson on two occasions. In his manor house, as a matter of fact. So, you see, there's this interesting triangle between the prince, the prince's best friend, and the London mafia."

"Interesting triangle, Briggs?"

"Well, I mean—"

"Look, Agent Briggs, I just took a call from the president's chief of staff. I'm to be at the White House this afternoon to brief POTUS on the kidnapping. Do you have *any idea* where the prince is?"

"Well, no sir, but—"

"Do you have any idea where Newton Dempsey is? Remember Newton Dempsey, Briggs? The kidnapper? The guy from Boston?"

"Chief, we're not needed for that. I'm sure MI5 is capable of following any leads Dempsey might have left behind. They know London better than I do, after all. But I've said it before and I'll say it again: Dempsey doesn't fit the crime. He doesn't, Chief. He just doesn't. There's got to be more to this. And I'm convinced, that is, Agent Kovalev and I are *both* convinced"—*strength in numbers*, Kori thought—"that this guy Quincy, who, by the way, was following *us* around, mind you, is somehow involved. And Holland, Grayson's best buddy, is involved with Quincy. From the Turner crime family, no less. What's the connection? I'll admit that right now, we haven't a clue. But somehow I just know it all fits together. And we have to follow up on it, don't we, Chief?"

Eaglethorpe was quiet for a moment, no doubt mulling over his top agent's appraisal of the situation. Finally, he said, "Look, Agent Briggs, can you give me *any*thing to tell the prez?"

"Well, you can tell him that we believe the kidnapping goes deeper than Dempsey and that perhaps Dempsey is partnered with known criminals. And tell him Agent Briggs says 'hey.'"

Eaglethorpe chuckled but covered his mouth to make sure Kori didn't hear it. "Okay, Briggs," he said. "But might I remind you that you have just two and a half days before Dempsey's deadline to kill the prince? It's getting late in the game."

"I know, Chief."

"So get to work."

"Yes, sir."

"And keep me posted."

"Of course."

Eaglethorpe paused and then quietly said, "I trust you, Kori."

Kori smiled. "I know, Chief. I won't let you down."

She hung up and turned to Anya. "Chief's getting a little antsy."

"I am sure."

"I know how he feels. He's got to tell the president something and, let's be honest, all we have so far are a bunch of riddles."

"Maybe Cooper will have something on Holland that we can use."

"Let's hope so. I guess we're dead in the water until then. When it gets right down to it, Holland is really our only decent lead right now."

"Kori, maybe we can make use of our time waiting for Cooper's report."

"A drink at the bar? Good thinking, Anya."

"Well, actually, I was thinking that perhaps we can check into Spenser Burke's death."

"Oh, well, that's not a bad idea either. Graham said they found his body in the Thames, but that's all we know. I'd be curious how he got there." She pulled out her phone and opened her map app. "There's a Metropolitan Police station on Savile Row. A ten-minute walk from here. Why don't we make an inquiry?"

"Do you think they will tell us anything?"

"Well, the death is public information, right? Maybe they can't tell us everything about the investigation, but we might learn something of interest. It's worth asking. Maybe we'll get lucky and the station sergeant will be a lonely guy only too happy to accommodate a couple of eye-batting females."

As it happened, the station sergeant was no such thing. The station sergeant was a happily married woman on whom eye-batting from two other women was lost. Nevertheless, because she was a public servant, she had no problem disclosing what the official record showed.

"Gunshot wound to the back of the head," she reported, standing behind the counter looking at a computer screen.

"He didn't drown?" Kori asked.

"No, ma'am. He was apparently dead long before being tossed into the river."

"Are you able to disclose any details on the investigation?" Anya asked. "Are there any suspects, for instance?"

"Well, of course, we rarely comment on ongoing investigations," the station sergeant replied. "But, as it happens, I can tell you that this particular investigation is closed."

"Closed?" Kori said. "How can that be? I mean, did they find the killer already?"

The desk sergeant looked closer at the screen and shook her head. "Don't know. It is strange, though. I was here when the call came in that the body was found. Obviously murdered. That normally marks the start of a very long and very comprehensive investigatory process. But there's nothing really here. Just an order for the case to be closed."

"Order from whom?"

"MI5, ma'am. They have ultimate jurisdiction. I'm sorry, did you know the poor bloke?"

"Sort of."

"I see. Well, I'm afraid I have no further information. Now, I reckon you can take it up with MI5 to see what they know or why they might have ordered the investigation closed, but I think you'll find they're a pretty tight-lipped bunch."

"Okay, well thank you, anyway," Kori said. The agents turned to go and Kori thought of one more question. "Officer, does it say who with MI5 ordered the case closed?"

The desk sergeant looked back at the screen. "An agent by the name of Graham, ma'am. Agent Victor Graham."

It was late in the afternoon and the agents were doing what Kori had earlier suggested. Having a drink in the hotel bar.

"That son of a bitch," Kori was saying. "The case isn't closed. It isn't closed at all. MI5 took it over and is working on it in secret. Graham probably knew we'd check with the police. I'll bet he closed the case even before he called me to tell me Burke was a dead end."

On a muted TV above the bar, a news report showed another picture of Dempsey, again with the caption "Person of interest." Then came a picture of the queen with its own caption: "Queen remains confident in investigation of missing son."

"So Burke is evidently not a dead end," Anya said.

"Nope. But God forbid that Graham should admit that to me. Now, we're not going to find out anything about Burke's death."

"Well, we know one thing, Kori."

"What's that?"

"He was killed by a bullet to the back of the head."

"Right. Execution style."

"Mob-style."

"Exactly."

Kori's phone buzzed. "The call we've been waiting for," she said. "Talk to me, Coop," she said into the phone. "What the scoop on our man Holland?"

"Well, Kori, I'm not sure what you expected, but the man is spotless. His finance company is clean and so is he. He's well-respected personally and professionally. He's married and has two grown children, one male, one female. He lives a quiet life and is rarely seen in public. He frequents Whites's, but you already knew that. He gives a lot of money to charity, and I mean *a lot*. Enough to get knighted, hence the "Sir" appellation. He started a charity foundation for orphans and the homeless about ten years ago, and today, his wife runs the day-to-day details of it. Holland keeps mostly to his business. Nose to the grindstone. Kori, I can't find anything negative about him. The man has never had so much as a parking ticket."

"Wow, Coop, *nothing*?"

"Nothing in his adult life."

"Hmm . . . well what about when he was younger?"

"Ah, well, that's where it gets interesting, Kori."

"Geez, Coop, you might have led with the interesting part."

"Sorry. But get this: we can find nothing on John Holland's life before the year 1988."

"What do you mean nothing? Nothing incriminating?"

"I mean nothing period. It's as if he just came out of nowhere sometime around his twentieth birthday. Like he was just beamed to this planet. No parents, no childhood home, no grade school records, not even a birth certificate. For all intents and purposes, the man didn't even exist before 1988."

"That can't be right, Coop."

"I had Foster digging, too. We came up empty."

"Well, where was he when the records of his life start showing up?"

"The trail starts at the University of Cambridge. John Holland was an economics student. After he graduated, he stuck around and earned a master's degree in finance. Then he went to London and began the life everybody knows about."

"And you can't trace him backward from Cambridge?"

"Kori, there *is* no John Holland before Cambridge."

"But, Coop, I'm sure he's been interviewed for magazines and TV. Profile pieces, right? Someone must have asked him about his childhood at some point."

"Yes, there have been several profile pieces that we uncovered. *Insider Magazine*, *Business Matters*, and other periodicals. The BBC did a piece on him a few years back. But he's always very vague about his background. He claims to have grown up in Canterbury, about sixty miles southeast of London. But we can find no records of him there. And in interviews, that's about all he says before changing the subject. Apparently, nobody's thought to dig any further. His life as an adult is all anyone wants to report about. People just want to know how he became so successful."

"That's beyond strange, Coop. It's downright suspicious."

"Indeed it is. Thirty-five years of details. And before that? Twenty years of total nonexistence."

# 16

The University of Cambridge was an hour-and-a-half drive from London, mostly on the M11, running north past English towns with names like Woodford, Chigwell, Elsenham, and Duxford. Once outside the city, the geography turned to fields and woods and gently sloping hills. The English sky was still largely overcast with the sun here and there poking through the clouds.

"I love the English countryside," Kori remarked as the agents drove toward their destination. "Peaceful, you know?"

Anya nodded from the driver's seat. "Yes, but let us hope there is more to this little side trip than the view."

"I hear ya. Well, we wouldn't even have to make this trip if student records prior to 1995 were digitized. I'd have Foster hack in and pull Holland's file and he'd have it to us in five minutes. But alas, such is not the case."

"Alas."

"All we need to see is his application, Anya. Holland is hiding something from his past. In fact, more than that, Holland is hiding everything from his past."

"And this has a bearing on the kidnapping of an English prince by an American how exactly?"

"Now you're starting to sound like the chief."

"Sorry, Kori, but you have to admit this seems like a long shot. Do not get me wrong. I am enjoying this lovely drive even if I cannot seem to escape the uncomfortable feeling that I am driving on the wrong side of the road."

"Speaking of which, here's some interesting trivia I'll bet you didn't know. The British drive on the left because medieval knights, riding on horseback, would always pass each other on the left. They wanted to be able to wield their swords in their right hands and give themselves the chance for a more direct swipe at the other, just in case the other rider was a foe, most knights being right-handed and all. So, when cars came along, it just seemed natural to continue the tradition."

"Hmm . . . I think I am calling bullshit on your trivia."

"You mean 'bollocks.'"

"I prefer my term."

"Either way, it's true. Look it up."

"I intend to. I do not pretend to be the history buff that you are, but it seems to me as if there was quite a period of time between the days of medieval knights and the days of the automobile. But you are changing the subject, my friend. The fact is, we are losing the rest of the day on this little excursion."

"I know, I know. But cripes, Anya, I just *know* that Holland is somehow involved in the kidnapping. He has to be. Don't you think so? Can't you just feel it?"

"I would say that, given his relationship with the prince and the connection of both he and the prince to Andrew Quincy, who is a member of the London mafia, and the mob-style hit on Burke, who was connected to Newton Dempsey, that it might be possible that Holland is, at the least—how do you say?—tangentially connected."

"Okay, then. Tangentially. Good enough. Now, nothing in his current life would seem to confirm that though, right? He's Mister Clean. Works hard, keeps to himself, even gives to charity. He's the kind of guy who would never travel in the same circles as Dempsey, Burke, or Quincy. But the man seemingly came out of the mist at the age of twenty. That's just plain bizarre. Who is he, really? I'm telling you, Anya, the answer is at the records department of the University of Cambridge."

"Perhaps. I will admit that it's worth following up on. But I fear the records department will be closed by the time we get there."

"We'll hit it first thing in the morning. So long as we can find a print shop that's open this evening, we'll be fine."

"And a restaurant."

"Right. And a restaurant."

The restaurant was a traditional country pub not too far from the university where the agents ordered quail with cornbread stuffing and a couple of local ales. Earlier, they'd checked in to the Gonville Hotel, an historic luxury hotel with a wellness spa that both agents lamented not having time for. Then they'd found their print shop and then made it to the pub.

Kori presented more trivia over dinner, including the fact that the university, founded in 1209, was the second-oldest university in the English-speaking world. It began when a group of scholars left the oldest university in the English-speaking world, Oxford, founded somewhere, it is generally thought, around 1096, and started their own university ninety miles away. It is believed Cambridge was where Isaac Newton sat under an apple tree, got bonked on the head by an apple that fell from said tree, and subsequently developed his theory of gravity.

"I believe I will call bullshit on that one, too," Anya declared.

"Well, it's more of a legend, I suppose," Kori said. "But how about this: did you know that the university has over a hundred libraries? And the central one alone has over eight million volumes?"

"That is a lot of books."

After a few more interesting and not-so-interesting pieces of trivia, a couple more ales, and dessert—roasted pear, carrot, and coconut cake, a house specialty—the agents retreated to the Gonville. They discussed the next morning's plan once more before going to their separate rooms with Kori promising that, yes, she'd do the talking at the records department. Anya was adamant that she herself could not pull off a British accent.

"Blimey," Kori said, "it's easy, innit? But don't you fret, mate. I'll be the cheeky one."

"If that means I do not have to speak tomorrow," said Anya, "then I am happy and I will say goodnight, my friend."

"Cheers, mate. Cor, I'm bloody knackered meself."

Kori called her mother from her room who informed Kori, after the usual niceties and catching up that, apparently, there were no further developments in the case of missing Prince Grayson, at least according to her online tabloid sources. "Well, keep me posted, Mom," Kori said, stifling a laugh. Her mother assured her that she would.

Promptly at 8:30 the next morning, with two days left before Dempsey's deadline, the agents arrived at the university's records department. Unlike the Metropolitan Police station, it looked as if they might have better luck. The attendant at the front desk was a young man this time, probably a graduate student, Kori surmised, tall and gangly and bespectacled. He was busy behind the counter, tapping away at his computer keyboard when the alluring women appeared in front of him.

"Excuse me," Kori said in her best British accent.

The young man looked up and involuntarily found himself, mouth open, moving his eyes from head to toe of the blonde and brunette that the universe had seen fit, for whatever reason, to place before him that morning. Then he caught himself and managed to say, "Yes, ma'am, can I help you?"

"My boss sent me here. We'd placed a request. I'm to pick up a copy of his student file. He graduated in 1991."

"Of course," said the young man. "And what's your boss's name?"

"John Holland. *Sir* John Holland."

This, too, took the young man aback. "Really? Sir John Holland, the rich guy? The billionaire?"

"That's the bloke."

The young man tapped away at his screen for a moment or two. Then he frowned and said, "I'm sorry, ma'am, but I don't see a request here."

"What? That's quite impossible. I made the request myself just yesterday."

"Oh, that explains it. All requests require forty-eight hours' notice, ma'am."

"Well nobody explained that to me. Oh, my. Sir John had us drive up special this morning. He's writing his memoirs, you see. There's a whole chapter on his time here at Cambridge. It was a very lovely time for him and he wants to make sure he gets the details right. You know, what courses he took, his extracurricular activities, who his professors were, and so forth. We need to get all the spellings correct, of course, and make sure everything is as accurate as possible."

"Yes, I see. Of course, that makes perfect sense. But, unfortunately, there's really nothing I can do. I'm very sorry. The request simply hasn't been processed through the system yet. Could you come back tomorrow?"

"Oh, no, that won't do. No, no, no. Sir John is not going to like this," Kori said, shaking her head. "Not going to like this at all. He's a donor, you know. A quite generous one at that. I'd hate to disappoint him."

The young man was quiet for a moment, apparently thinking things over. Evidently unable to resolve the matter in his mind, he said at last, "I'd like to help, but there are rules, you know?"

"Quite right. But aren't rules sometimes made to be broken? Or at least bent a little? Hmm?"

"Well, begging your pardon, ma'am, but I'm not even sure you're who you say you are. No offense, of course, but how do I know you even work for Sir John Holland?"

"Oh, sorry, my mistake, I'm sure," said Kori, digging into her pocketbook. "I should have given you this straight away." She handed him one of the business cards she and Anya had printed the evening before, a heavy, off-white linen number with silver foil embossed text.

*Kelly Bridges, Executive Personal Secretary to Sir John Holland, JEH Financial Group, London, UK.*

"And this is my assistant, Amy," she added.

Anya nodded toward the young man and said, "Cheers, mate," while Kori tried not to laugh out loud.

"Well, even still, I probably shouldn't—"

"Young man," Kori smiled disarmingly. "May I have your name?"

"My name, ma'am?"

"For the acknowledgments page of the book, of course. Sir John Holland likes to show his appreciation."

"Really?" The young man smiled in return. "My name is Lucas King, ma'am. K-I-N-G."

"Well, you know, Lucas King, K-I-N-G, you seem very diligent in your work. Sir John appreciates diligence. Holds it in very high regard, he does. When you graduate, I might recommend you come 'round to JEH. I'm sure I can convince the man to spend a few minutes with you."

"Me? A meeting with Sir John Holland?"

"Indeed. Perhaps we'll even have a situation for you."

"Wow, that would be . . . amazing," Lucas King beamed.

"Now, in the meantime, if you could just see your way to allowing us to take a look at Sir John's file."

Lucas looked around furtively and said, "Well, I can't let you make a copy of it," he said, "but you can look through it. Is that okay?"

"I suppose it'll have to do, won't it?" Kori replied.

"Wait here. I'll be right back." And then Lucas went through a door that presumably led to the room where the records were archived.

Kori turned to Anya. "'Cheers, mate'?"

"Did I not sound sufficiently British?"

Kori laughed. "You sounded sufficiently Russian trying to sound British."

Fifteen minutes later, Lucas returned with a manilla folder. "Now, you can't take it out of here," he said, "but you're welcome to have a seat over at that table and look through it. I'm afraid that's the best I can do."

"Thank you, Lucas," said Kori, taking the file. "You're a good bloke."

The agents sat down at the table Lucas had pointed to and began leafing through the file but they didn't get any further than Holland's initial application before they both did a double-take.

"Anya," Kori whispered, "no wonder his name doesn't pop up anywhere before the age of twenty."

"Because John Holland was not his name," Anya whispered back.

"He changed it."

"Indeed he did."

"And his original name is much more interesting, wouldn't you agree?"

Anya nodded. "Turner," she said. "John Turner from London."

**17**

—·—

From 1950 to 1967, the Kray brothers, identical twins Reginald and Ronald, were the preeminent leaders of organized crime in London. Operating from the city's East End, their gang, called simply The Firm, ran protection rackets and all manner of illegal enterprises. Among other nefarious activities, they were tied to murders, hijackings, and armed robberies. The Krays opened a nightclub, too, called Esmeralda's Barn, and were part of the swinging London social scene of the 1960s. The brothers became rich. They could be charming and acquired a sort of celebrity status. You can find pictures of them from those days socializing with the likes of Frank Sinatra, Sammy Davis Jr., Peter Sellers, Liza Minelli, and various British politicians. Eventually, they were arrested and, with several of their gang members taking plea deals for testifying against them, were convicted of murder and given life sentences.

At that point, several gangs jumped in to fill the criminal void left by the Krays, each jostling for position. Among them was a small criminal enterprise run by an East End thug named Finley Turner. Finley had been a hit man with another gang, then started his own when he felt as if the boss, the notorious Ralphy "Sledgehammer" Gills, cheated him out of some pay. Gills got his nickname from the tool he used to kill *his* former boss. Finley Turner just used a gun, fatally shooting Gills as he left his London townhome one morning. Then, with Gills's gang in disarray, Finley started what would eventually become the Turner crime empire. For the most part, Finley did it ruthlessly, and for that, hired the most sociopathic gangsters he could find, poaching them from other gangs with promises of wealth.

For several years after the Krays' ignominious fall, it was all-out war around London, the frequency of assassinations rivaling Chicago's mob wars of the 1930s. But by the late 1970s, the Turner mob was the undisputed leader of gangland London. Finley kept the promises to his employees, paying them handsomely and, sociopathic or not, they remained unquestionably loyal.

Finley's son, Harry, came into the business in the 1980s, pretty much taking over in the '90s as the old man's health gradually deteriorated. Finley died of heart failure in 1994, having never served a day in prison for his crimes. Harry hadn't intended to serve a day either, but his methodology was different. Where Finley used ruthlessness, Harry used cunning and smarts. The world was changing and he knew it. He wanted to run more than a local mob with its hands into pedestrian vices like gambling and numbers and prostitution. He courted international business, importing stolen goods, counterfeit merchandise, and drugs—cocaine, heroin, and crystal meth. He expanded operations to include most of the United Kingdom, worming his mob into previously untouchable places like Liverpool and Glasgow, each with their own entrenched organized crime families. But Harry avoided the gangland wars. He made deals with the other families, forming imposing and highly profitable cartels. Everyone enjoyed the spoils.

In 1968, Harry had a son named John, an apparent heir to the family business. John lived the relatively normal life of a boy in London and then went off to the University of Cambridge. That's when the record of his life seems to have simply stopped.

Rampart agent Darren Cooper was explaining all this to Kori as she and Anya spoke to him on the phone from Kori's room back at the Gonville. Director Eaglethorpe was on the line, too.

"But Coop," Kori said, "why has nobody traced John Turner to John Holland?"

"Two reasons, I would guess," Cooper replied. "First, nobody's ever thought to. All eyes have been on Harry Turner. Plus, there's another son—Lennox Turner, and it's generally accepted that Lennox is now running things. Second, even if they'd wanted to trace John Turner, we can assume that his name was changed fraudulently. Nobody could connect Turner with Holland because there's no official record of the change. For whatever reason, John wanted to disassociate from his father's business. Or maybe he wanted to leave the family altogether, who knows? With his connections, I'm sure it would have been easy enough for him to find a decent counterfeiter, so he could've had new IDs printed and then went to the student affairs office at Cambridge one day where he was enrolled and told them he was now officially John Holland. They changed his file, and from then on, that's who he was. In other words, the only record in existence that ties John Turner with John Holland is that file you saw in the records department, a file I'll bet nobody's opened since Holland's graduation. Who would have had any need to? And as you discovered, it takes a personal visit and a little deception to gain access to it."

"Okay," Eaglethorpe said, "so maybe it's hard to connect Holland with Turner, but someone would have investigated John Turner's life after college, right? He's the son of a mob leader. I mean, suddenly, he just disappears?"

"Yeah, we did some digging on that, too, Chief," said Cooper. "We can't find anything officially on record anywhere, but apparently, word went out on the street that Harry's son John was the victim of a drug overdose while away at Cambridge. Supposedly there was a memorial service back in London and the family even went into a period of mourning. So John Turner never returning to London was perfectly believable."

"But, Coop," said Kori. "He *did* return. He returned as John Holland. Certainly, someone would have recognized him."

"First of all, Kori, John Holland seems to never have traveled even remotely in the same circles as his father or brother. Nobody he's dealt with seems at all connected with the Turner crime family. At least publicly. Second of all, for anyone who might notice a resemblance, I'm guessing a little plastic surgery would have been sufficient to throw them off the track. Plus, London's a big city. He could move to a different section and never be discovered by old acquaintances. And of course now thirty-five years have come and gone. He's going to look a lot different, no matter what."

"So why would he do it, Coop?"

"Evidently, he wanted to divorce himself entirely from the family business."

"There might be another reason," Anya offered. "Perhaps he wanted to *expand* the family business."

"How so, Agent Kovalev?" Eaglethorpe asked.

"Well, without the last name of Turner, he would be much freer than his father or brother to operate, yes?"

"I can see that," said Kori. "JEH could be a front for God knows what kinds of illegal enterprises with the Turner family working behind the scenes. Meanwhile, Holland cultivates the persona of a well-respected businessman and philanthropist. He even becomes knighted. Oh, man, it's brilliant."

"If you're right, ladies," Cooper said, "then JEH may well be providing the cover for one of the largest criminal enterprises on the planet. It's a billion-dollar private company. You could run millions of dollars of illegal activity through it and nobody would notice."

"So Holland is a legitimate businessman in his own right," said Kori. "Highly successful. But he's also a highly successful illegitimate businessman."

"Entirely plausible," Cooper agreed.

"But, people, you're forgetting one thing," said Eaglethorpe. "Legitimate or not, tied to the Turners or not, we have no evidence whatsoever that John Holland is a kidnapper. Of a prince. Who's a friend of his."

"A friend who owes him a lot of money," Kori said.

"Even still, Agent Briggs. What's six hundred thousand pounds to a guy like Holland? Why take such a risk?"

"I hear you, Chief. I guess the mystery remains."

"And need I remind you that we still haven't found a way to tie Newton Dempsey into any of this?"

"No, but it's possible to imagine Spenser Burke tied to Holland," offered Cooper. "Burke was a known white-collar criminal. He might have had contacts with the mob. And then maybe Burke recruited Dempsey."

"But why, Agent Cooper? How could Burke have even known Dempsey? A guy out of prison in England recruits a guy out of prison in the US? As if there's some club somewhere where ex-prisoners from all over the world meet every Tuesday night? How could they have possibly ever come across each other?"

"I see what you mean, Chief."

"Look, Agents Briggs and Kovalev, your discovery is obviously not without value. I'm not necessarily seeing how it helps with the investigation of Prince Grayson's kidnapping, but it's important for its own sake if nothing else. Get yourselves back to London ASAP, take what you've uncovered, and deliver it to MI5."

"Ugh," Kori mumbled.

"Excuse me, Agent Briggs?"

"Oh, nothing, Chief. Let's just say I'm not exactly on the best of terms with my contact there."

"I know, but it doesn't matter. We have a duty to report this information to them whether we like it or not."

"I understand."

"And after that, get back to the subject at hand. The reason you're over there: Prince Grayson. What's your next step?"

Kori looked at Anya and both shrugged simultaneously. "Well, um, we're working on it, Chief," said Kori. "You can be sure of that."

"I certainly hope so, Agent Briggs. I'll be awaiting an update."

"Roger that, Chief."

Everyone hung up and Kori turned to Anya. "Well, you heard the chief, my Russian friend. Let's get on with the next step."

"You do not know what that is, do you, my American friend?"

"Oh, I know. Do you know?"

"Of course I do. I just want to make sure you know."

"Don't worry about me. I know exactly what the next step is."

"Good. That makes two of us."

"Yes, good."

But both agents knew only one thing: neither had a clue of what the next step was.

Kori had taken several photos of John Holland's—née John Turner's—student file with her cell phone and transferred them to her tablet, which she was showing MI5 agent Victor Graham. The two were sitting at the Coburg Bar in the Connaught. Anya and Kori had driven back to London from Cambridge and Kori called Graham along the way to inform him that she had yet more vital information to pass along. Not that she had wanted to. But Eaglethorpe made it clear that MI5 had a right to know about the double life of John Holland, especially since there was a possibility that Holland might somehow be involved in the kidnapping of the prince. Graham had sounded skeptical, even hesitant, but agreed to meet with her. "Where are you staying now?" he'd asked. And then they'd agreed to meet in the Coburg.

Graham was nursing a gin and tonic. Kori was drinking a Scotch.

"Well, of course, this is all very interesting," Graham had to admit, looking at the photos. "Your investigative efforts are apparently not without merit." Kori rolled her eyes as Graham continued. "As it happens, we have an organized crime task force in place. The head of it is a personal friend of mine. I will most certainly pass this information along to him."

"You might want to also pass along that Andrew Quincy works for John Holland."

"Oh? Is that right?"

"Yes, that's right. It turns out that he doesn't work at White's as you'd said."

"Well, I—"

"Look, don't bother to explain, Graham. You didn't know who Quincy was and you were too embarrassed to say so. Either that or you were purposely withholding information from me. Probably the latter, but definitely one of the two, and I'm not sure which is worse."

"I hardly think—"

Kori interrupted him. "It doesn't matter. I'm here because my boss insists I share this information with you, so let's just move past it so I can get on with what's left of my evening. Now, maybe you've done some digging on Quincy since I gave you his name. I hope so. If you have, then you know he works for a company called Hudson Imports, a front for a counterfeit merchandise operation. What you may not know is that he meets with Holland personally."

Graham took a swallow of his gin and tonic. "Well, as I said, Ms. Briggs, I will pass this information along to my friend with the organized crime task force. Perhaps he will be in touch with you."

"Need I remind you, Graham, that there are implications here concerning the prince? Quincy was seen in Grayson's company on two occasions shortly before the kidnapping."

"Meaning what, exactly?"

"You don't find that interesting?"

"Are you seriously suggesting that the Turner crime family is somehow involved in the kidnapping plot, Ms. Briggs? That seems highly unlikely."

"Prince Grayson owed Holland's company over six hundred thousand pounds."

"Holland is a billionaire. That's a pittance."

Kori took a swallow of her Scotch. This is the point at which she and Anya had been stuck. Yes, there was a connection between the London mob and the prince's kidnapping. No, there wasn't a rational explanation for it.

"Well, nevertheless," Kori finally said, "I would think you'd be interested in following up on every lead, wouldn't you?"

"Every reasonable one."

"Look, I know you have no interest in taking advice from me, Graham, but if I were you—in charge of finding the prince before the deadline runs out—and I hadn't found him yet, I'd consider the unreasonable leads, too. Now, I'm here with my partner and we don't have the manpower, but your organization ought to be tailing Holland and Quincy everywhere they go. That seems like a no-brainer to me."

Graham smiled politely. Too politely. "Well, thank you so very much for your advice, Agent Briggs. I will most certainly consider it and give it all the attention it most assuredly deserves."

Kori chuckled. "I'll tell ya, there's no sarcasm like British sarcasm."

"Is that quite all, Ms. Briggs? I would hate to keep you from, as you say, what's left of your evening."

"That's everything, Mr. Graham. I did what I promised my boss I would do."

"Then I will say good evening."

"Good evening."

# 18

—·—

"It's the guy's arrogance that really irritates me. You can't tell him anything. It's infuriating." Kori was explaining to Anya how the meeting with Graham had gone. "I even had to pay the tab again."

"Bastard!" Anya said. "Just when I imagined things could not get any lower."

"Right?"

The pair were in Anya's hotel room. It was getting late and dusk was settling over the city of London. Anya had called the Connaught Grill for room service and was enjoying the Welsh lamb while Kori savored the Dover sole. Both helped themselves to the bottle of French Bordeaux Anya had ordered with the meals.

"Anya, we need a plan. I mean, we have to do something. I suggested to Graham that he ought to follow Quincy and Holland around. He's not going to do it, so why don't we?"

"It will be hard to follow both."

"Well, then, maybe we ought to just pick one. Holland's the leader of the outfit. Let's focus on him."

"But, Kori, I think we got lucky following Holland to that pub. In every organization, there are brains and there is brawn. Brains normally keep themselves above the fray. Insulated from the real action. Brawn is where everything happens."

"So you're saying we should follow Quincy?"

"I think he is more likely to lead us somewhere productive. For all we know, he may lead us to the prince."

"Something tells me it can't possibly be that easy, but okay, let's go back to Hudson Imports first thing in the morning and start tailing Quincy."

"Excellent."

The two ate in silence for a bit and then Kori grabbed the bottle of Bordeaux and refilled their glasses. "Say, Anya," she grinned, "who's the brains and who's the brawn in our little outfit?"

"Between you and me?"

"Between you and me."

"It is obvious, is it not?"

"Yes," Kori said. "Quite obvious."

"Yes, quite obvious," Anya agreed.

Neither agent could help smiling.

Back in her room, Kori decided to call her mother. Normally when she was on assignment, she enjoyed the calls to Joan and a large part of the enjoyment was that the conversations took her mind off her work. Speaking with her mother grounded her somehow. Not so with the case of the missing prince. It was all Joan seemed to want to talk about.

"Have you heard the latest rumor, Kori?"

Kori sighed. "No, Mom, what's the latest rumor?"

"He's run off with his girlfriend!"

"The prince had a girlfriend?"

"A secret girlfriend. She's a dancer at a club. Can you believe it? Twenty-two years old."

"*Star Globe* again, Mom?"

"Kori, they're an excellent source of news. Remember that story about Leonardo DiCaprio?"

"Yes, I remember. DiCaprio sued them for libel, as I recall."

"But they settled out of court, Kori. What does *that* tell you?"

Kori figured there was nothing to do but humor Joan. "So the prince ran off with a twenty-two-year-old club dancer? Where to?"

"Rumor has it they're in Finland."

"Finland, Mom?"

"Yes. Someone spotted them at the Helsinki Railway Station. Isn't that something?"

"It sure is . . . something."

"They're supposedly very much in love, Kori."

"Uh-huh."

"But of course, they have to keep their love affair a secret. It would be quite the scandal."

"Of course."

"Prince Grayson rented her an apartment not far from his home so they could see each other more often. But now, he's decided to risk everything and run away with her. Frankly, I don't know what to think about it. I suppose it's kind of romantic. But a club dancer? For a prince?"

"Yes, what is one to think?"

The conversation continued for another ten minutes and then Kori, calculating that it was about 6 p.m. in Boston, told Joan that her boss was meeting her for dinner. "I'd love to hear more, Mom, but I better go. Can't be late for the boss. Love you." She hung up and then slipped into bed, chuckling at the thought of Prince Grayson and a twenty-two-year-old dancer making their way through the Helsinki Railway Station.

She woke up before daybreak realizing that Newton Dempsey's deadline was now just one day away. And she hadn't slept particularly well. With each passing hour of the night, the idea of following Andrew Quincy around began to seem less and less promising. By morning, it seemed like a complete waste of time, but what other options did they have?

Kori rose, made some coffee with the room's coffeemaker, and took a quick shower. She dressed and looked at her watch. She was due to meet Anya in the lobby for breakfast in an hour and decided to kill the time by going for a walk outside. The sun had just come up. It was a crisp, gray morning and she walked down Mount

Street, known for its high-end stores. Nothing was open yet but Kori window-shopped past a jewelry boutique, a women's clothing store, and a Christian Louboutin shoe store. She crossed Audley Street and walked another block before deciding to head back to the hotel.

As she turned around, she noticed a man ducking into a doorway about fifty yards away in the direction of the hotel. She took a few steps toward him. Realizing he'd been spotted, the man began to run away.

"Hey!" Kori yelled, running after him, "stop!"

She picked up her pace and so did the man. He turned the corner back at the Connaught and ran a block to Adam's Row where he took a left and ran another block. Kori kept gaining on him. Fifty yards' distance between them became thirty, which became twenty, and then fifteen. Adam's Row led back to Audley and then Aldford Street. The man darted into an alley off Aldford, but the alley led to a tall, chain-link fence. He was trapped.

The man stopped and turned around. Kori drew her Glock and pointed it at him, walking slowly toward him and catching her breath. The man raised his hands.

"Okay, who are you?" Kori demanded. "And why are you following me?"

The man said nothing. Kori was about to ask again, more forcefully, when she felt a sudden blow to the back of her head. Everything lit up at once, as if a flash of lightning had burst in front of her eyes. And then, just as quickly, everything went black.

"Miss?"

Kori lifted her head and felt a sharp pain at the back of her skull, surging up to her temple, and then pounding on her forehead. She put her hand to the back of her head and felt the rise of a nasty welt. How did that get there? And where in the world was she? Somewhere on a street, she thought. Yes, some street in London, England. That seemed right. But why was she lying on the ground?

"Miss?"

And who was this man leaning over her?

"Miss?" the man repeated. "Are you okay?"

Through the fog in her brain, Kori managed to pull herself together and sit up. She looked around. Right—she'd chased someone into this alley. She had pulled her Glock. She glanced around her. The gun was gone. *Damn!* She remembered asking the man she'd been chasing who he was. That was right before the lights had gone out.

"An ambulance is on its way," the man leaning over her was saying.

She looked closer. The man—not a bad-looking man, as a matter of fact— was in uniform, the unmistakable uniform of a London police officer with the unique red and white checkered band around the hat. According to the stripes on his sleeve, the man was a sergeant, no less.

"No, Sergeant," Kori said. "No ambulance. Please, I'm fine." To prove it, she stood, wobbling a little at first, but then regaining her balance.

"I don't know, miss," the sergeant said, rising from his kneeling position beside her, "We'll let the EMTs have a look at you."

"Seriously, there's really no need, Sergeant . . . ?"

"Willis, ma'am. Sergeant Fletcher Willis. At your service." Kori stepped back and got a better look at Sergeant Fletcher Willis. Tall, broad-shouldered, chiseled face with hazel eyes. And, no wedding ring. Not that it mattered. It was merely one of those observations an intelligence agent is trained to make.

"Sergeant Willis, did you happen to see a man run from here?"

"Three men, I should say, miss."

"Kori." She extended her hand. "Kori Briggs."

The sergeant shook Kori's hand and smiled briefly. "American?"

Kori nodded.

"Ms. Briggs, I do have to insist that you tell me what happened here."

"I was hoping you'd tell *me*, Sergeant Fletcher," Kori said, ignoring his last name. "You see, I chased a man into here—"

"Wait, *you* chased *him*?" Willis took out a notepad.

"That's right. Then I approached him," *best to leave the gun out of it, for the time being*, Kori thought, "to find out who he was. And then I was apparently beaned on the back of the head."

"Yes, well, it must have been at that moment that I came by," said Willis. "Three men were leaning over you and it looked as though two of them were getting ready to pick you up and carry you off. I shouted to them. One of them pulled a gun." *probably my Glock!* Kori thought. "And I took cover over there behind that rubbish bin. Then, you see, they all jumped into a waiting car and sped off. I got the license plate and called it in right after I called for an ambulance. We'll get them, Ms. Briggs, I assure you. Now, who *was* this man you were chasing and why were you chasing him?"

"Well, he was following me. As to who he was, as I said, that's what I was trying to find out." Kori thought for a moment and came to the only logical conclusion. She pulled out her phone and showed Willis a picture of Andrew Quincy. "The three men you saw . . . was one of them this guy?"

"Yes. That's the chap with the gun."

"Well, no offense, Sergeant Fletcher, but you're not going to get these guys. They're miles away by now, probably hiding out in a place so secret that nobody could find them."

"Are they indeed? Well, in that case, Ms. Briggs, I'm afraid that after you're cleared at hospital, I'll need you to report straightaway to the station to fill out a complete report. Obviously, we're going to have a lot of questions we'll need you to answer."

"No can do, Sergeant. No hospital, no station, no questions. I'm very sorry. I'm not trying to be difficult, but you see, I'm a law enforcement officer myself. On a case. A pretty important one. And I don't have any time to lose."

"I see. And just whom do you work for?"

"An American intelligence unit. I'm afraid that's all I can tell you. But you're welcome to verify my story with Agent Victor Graham of MI5." Twice she'd gone to that well if one counted the name-drop at the front entrance of White's. At Kingsley Moore's door, Graham's name had worked. But she knew this time was different. Sergeant Fletcher Willis wouldn't take her word for it as Moore had. He'd actually call Graham. And what would Graham say? He'd have to confirm her story. He couldn't dare take the chance of leaving her out to dry. Ignoring her was one thing, but actually impeding her movements and getting her bogged down in the police investigation of a random, back-alley attack would have repercussions that would involve Graham's superior and the president of the United States.

"Very good, Miss Briggs," Willis said with a skeptical look. "I will do just that. Please have a seat and I'll be back with you." Kori sat on the curb as Willis pulled out his phone and made a call. He sauntered off several yards and Kori could hear him on his phone, though she couldn't make out what was being said. About that time, the ambulance pulled up with its iconic British two-tone siren blaring. The siren stopped and two EMTs got out. Willis, still talking on the phone, waved them over toward Kori.

"What seems to be the problem, ma'am?" one of them asked her.

"Nothing at all, actually," Kori replied. "The good sergeant has overreacted, I'm afraid. I stumbled and hit my head, but it's nothing, I assure you."

"Where'd you hit, ma'am?"

Kori showed the EMT the back of her head, pulling her long hair aside.

"You stumbled *backwards*?"

"Crazy, huh?"

"That's quite a bump, ma'am."

"I've had worse."

He pulled out a penlight and looked in her eyes and then told her to follow his finger as he moved it back and forth.

"See? I'm fine."

"Any blurry vision?"

"Nope."

"Nausea?"

"None."

"Who's the president of the United States?"

"Herbert Hoover."

The EMT chuckled. "Well, you seem okay. We can't make you come with us, of course, but it might be a good idea to get checked out just the same."

"Thanks, but as I explained to the sergeant, I'm on a bit of a tight schedule."

The EMT looked at his partner, shrugged, and turned back to Kori. "Okay, ma'am, but if you start feeling out of sorts, don't hesitate to get checked out. Concussions can be serious."

"Understood. I will. And thank you."

Sergeant Willis hung up and walked back over to Kori as the ambulance pulled away. Fortunately, Kori's calculations about Graham had been correct.

"Well, Ms. Briggs, it seems as if you're free to go."

"Thank you, Sergeant."

"I was unable to get ahold of Agent Graham, but someone on his staff vouched for you. They wouldn't say, however, what it is you're investigating exactly."

"And you'd like to know."

"I must admit I'm curious," Willis said with a slight smile. "An American woman chases a man into a London alley, takes a poke on the back of the head, almost gets taken away, and tells me she's on what I can only assume is an international crime case. Yes, I'd like to know."

"I wish I could tell you, Sergeant Fletcher. Say, can I call you Fletch?"

"If you absolutely must."

"Well, Fletch, maybe I can tell you when the case is resolved. I hope very shortly."

"I happen to know that Graham is spearheading the task force investigating the disappearance of the prince."

"Oh? Is that so?"

"Might I be so bold as to ask if your appearance here has something to do with that?"

"As they say, Fletch, I can neither confirm nor deny."

"I see," Willis smiled.

"The larger point, for now, is that I owe you a debt of gratitude. You might possibly have saved my life by your arrival. And you could have been hurt or worse. I thank you and the US government thanks you."

"All in a day's work, miss."

"Kori."

"All in a day's work, Kori."

"I'm sure. Nevertheless, will you let me buy you a drink when I'm done with my case before I pop back across the pond? It's the very least I can do."

Willis grinned and Kori caught a playful twinkle in his eyes. "Well, I suppose it would be rude if I didn't accept your offer."

"Quite."

"We members of the London police are representatives of our fair city, and it wouldn't do to not represent her fairly." Willis dug a card out of his pocket and handed it to Kori. "You can reach me at this number," he said. "I'll very much look forward to it."

"Me too."

"If I can make a suggestion in the meantime, Ms. Briggs . . ."

"Of course."

"Put some ice on that bump of yours and be careful chasing strange men into alleys."

"Noted, Sergeant Willis."

Kori arrived back in the lobby of the Connaught and saw Anya pacing and drinking a cup of coffee.

"Kori!" Anya said, marching over to her, "where have you been? I have been waiting for you."

"Well—"

"Oh, please do not tell me you were out window shopping. Ah, my American friend, do you not realize we are down to merely one day? There is no time for frivolity! Come on."

She strode out of the lobby and into the street. Kori followed, chuckling to herself and rubbing the back of her head.

"I still don't understand why this man Andrew Quincy is so interested in us," Anya said. Kori had followed her out of the Connaught and stopped her just as she was about to wave down a taxicab. She explained what happened and the two went back inside the hotel. Kori managed to snag a couple of aspirins from the front desk clerk for her splitting headache, then the two agents sat down at a small table at the far end of the lobby to figure out their next move.

"Well, he obviously knows who we are and why we're in London," Kori said. "That much seems certain."

"But how did he find us here? Kori, we have been so careful about our movements since we checked out of the Savoy. We have not been followed, I am sure of it. And nobody knows we are here at the Connaught."

"Almost nobody," Kori said thoughtfully. "I can think of one person who knows. I had a drink with him here just last night, as a matter of fact."

"Kori, what are you saying?"

"Correct me if I'm wrong, but he is also the only one in London who knows what it is we are investigating. The only one who's known from the moment my plane touched down at Heathrow. Oh, it's all starting to fit together. Don't you see?"

"Kori. You are saying that MI5 agent Victor Graham is somehow involved with Quincy? That is quite a bold statement. I know you do not care for this man, but—"

"Anya, think about it. What other explanation is there for him being so obstinate about sharing information? *Any* information. Or for closing the case on Burke, for that matter. Why would he do that? 'You can go back to America now,' he told me. Sure, I'll bet he'd love that."

"But you heard Cooper. Twenty-five years of service. Decorations and medals. Even from the queen. 'Top-shelf,' Cooper called him."

"Look, I know it's hard to believe, but when you consider everything, Anya, it's the only thing that makes sense. He lied about Quincy, remember? Told me he worked at White's. We figured it was because he was embarrassed that I had uncovered a name he hadn't. That it was just a bruised ego. But that wasn't it at all. He knew the name, after all! I told him 'Quincy' but it was Graham who told me 'Andrew.' He just didn't want us investigating Quincy. And then closing the Burke case? It wasn't just to us. I'll bet he closed it to everybody. He doesn't want *anyone* prying into it. He's sabotaging the investigation, Anya. And when we met last night, he insisted on meeting me here. 'Where are you staying now?' he'd asked. Anya, how did he know we were no longer at the Savoy? Hmm? *How?*"

Anya was quiet, reflecting on Kori's observations. Finally, she said, "Okay, so if Graham is involved with Quincy, he might be involved with the London mafia."

"Yes."

"But even if that is true, we still do not have a connection to the kidnapping."

"Except that Quincy is supposedly a friend of the prince. That's all we've ever had. Well, that and the IOUs to Holland, whose name just happens to be Turner. But now we have something else."

"Which is?"

"The fact that Graham has been impeding our investigation into the kidnapping. You can't deny it, right? So why has he been doing that? And why send Quincy to follow us? I'll tell you why. Because Graham is involved with it!"

"I do not know, Kori. Everything you are saying makes sense, but—"

"We've got to call the chief, Anya. We can't sit on this. It needs to be known that the very person who is in charge of the investigation into the kidnapping of the prince might well be involved with the kidnappers!"

Director Richard Eaglethorpe was not convinced, bringing up Anya's objection.

"Agent Briggs, even if what you are saying is correct, even if Graham is somehow affiliated with the London mafia, we still do not have a direct connection between the mafia and the kidnapping. I'm not saying you're wrong; I'm just saying that the connection isn't there."

Kori and Anya were still at the table in the lobby, but now Kori was on the phone to HQ. The throbbing in her head was starting to disappear, or maybe she just wasn't noticing it anymore.

"So why has Graham continually blocked our investigation?" she asked. "From the very beginning."

"A connection that is *not* circumstantial. Look, Kori, I hear what you are saying. But this is a very serious charge and one that has to be backed up with real, verifiable evidence. Something tangible and not just a loose affiliation of happenstances. Besides which, you still haven't connected *any* of this to Newton Dempsey."

"Maybe not, but Chief, listen, tomorrow is the deadline. Someone has to tell the PM that the exact wrong person is leading his country's investigation."

"Not without evidence, Agent Briggs," Eaglethorpe repeated.

"There's no time, Chief. And the prince's life is hanging in the balance."

Eaglethorpe was quiet for a moment, contemplating the options. "Look, here's what we'll do," he said at last. "MI5 is not the only game in town. A member of the royal family has been kidnapped. You don't think every agency in the country is working on that? MI5 is the public face of the investigation, but I'm very sure that MI6 is busy on it, too, in their own way. As it happens, I have a contact there. An old friend of mine. Let me make a phone call and set up a meeting for you. We probably should have done that sooner, but I was reluctant to circumvent the people the president set us up with. At least without good cause."

"So you believe me."

"I didn't say that. But you definitely have some information that someone independent from MI5 ought to be informed about. We have a duty to pass that information along, regardless of its current state of provability. At the same time, maybe you can learn what MI6 knows. That certainly couldn't hurt. In my estimation, the huge missing piece to this puzzle is Newton Dempsey's connection. Agreed?"

"Agreed."

"All this other stuff is interesting, perhaps even relevant, but it's not getting us any closer to finding Dempsey and, therefore, the prince."

"Of course."

"So sit tight. Let me make a phone call to my friend and get you in there. I'll get right back to you."

SIS, the UK's Secret Intelligence Service, commonly referred to as MI6, was formed in 1909 and grew by leaps and bounds during the Second World War when it was part of the Directorate of Military Intelligence, a department of the British War Office. It was Section 6 of the Directorate, hence, the MI6 abbreviation. The agency was instrumental in code-breaking during the war. So secretive was MI6, that its existence wasn't even acknowledged until 1994. Today, the agency continues to deal almost exclusively with foreign intelligence, but when a prince goes missing, it's all hands on deck. Eaglethorpe was right; MI6 had their own investigation underway.

The SIS building was in Vauxhall, a twenty-minute drive from the Connaught. It rested on the Thames and looked like a fortress. Kori and Anya had to go through three different security checkpoints before they could be escorted to the office of Chief Security Officer Bentley Hayes, Eaglethorpe's contact.

Hayes, tall and solid with salt and pepper hair and friendly eyes, was keenly interested in the information the Rampart agents had to offer. *Finally*, Kori thought. It felt good to be heard. She and Anya were sitting across from Hayes at a rather large desk in his corner office looking over the river.

"I only wish we had more for *you*," Hayes said. "Frankly, we're hitting dead ends. It's been frustrating, to say the least. But this London mafia angle is intriguing. And worth pursuing, if you ask me." He spoke into his intercom. "Reynolds, come in here, please."

Presently a lean, pretty woman, probably around thirty, entered the office. "Leila Reynolds, these are US intelligence agents Kori Briggs and Anya Kovalev."

"Pleased, I'm sure," the woman said.

"They have some interesting information that may or may not have a bearing on the kidnapping. I'll explain it all later. For now, I want us to begin surveilling John Holland."

The woman's eyes widened. "*Sir* John Holland?"

"One and the same. And I want a tail put on someone else, too."

"Yes, sir?"

"Agent Victor Graham of MI5."

The woman's eyes widened a second time. "Begging your pardon, sir, but you mean for us to spy on an MI5 agent?"

"That's precisely what I mean. And put our best operatives on it. Pronto, Reynolds."

"Yes, sir. Straightaway, sir."

Leila Reynolds scurried out of the office. Hayes leaned back in his chair. "So how is Richard doing, anyway?" he asked.

"Director Eaglethorpe is doing just fine, sir," Kori replied.

"We worked together years ago, you know. Richard was stationed in Amsterdam."

"Actually, he's told us very little about his past."

"Amsterdam," Hayes repeated, looking off into the distance and smiling. "My goodness, those were some jolly good times." Then he caught himself and shook off his reverie. "I met him in Romania, you know. We were both sent there in 1989 by our respective agencies to get a handle on what became known as the Romanian Revolution. The people were rebelling against communism, like much of Eastern Europe at the time. This was only a couple of years before the fall of the Soviet Union. It was a time of great change. I'm sure you two were just children. Anyway, the leader of Romania was a dictator named Nicolae Ceaușescu."

"Yes, I have read about him," Anya said. "When his government was overthrown, Ceaușescu was executed by the people."

"On Christmas Day," Hayes added. "Your boss and I were there."

"I am sure it must have been fascinating to watch as history played itself out in those years," Anya remarked.

"Indeed it was."

"I'd like to get back to your time in Amsterdam, sir," Kori smiled impishly.

"Ha! I'll bet you would. Well, it was a long time ago and it's probably best if we leave it there. But I will say this: your chief is a damn good fellow."

"No argument there, sir," Kori said.

"The thing about Romania that was so interesting was that Ceaușescu ran a police state and he tried to censor all news coming from other Eastern European countries, but he couldn't—yes, Reynolds?"

The agents turned to see Leila Reynolds in the doorway.

"Begging your pardon, sir," she said, "but we have some news on MI5 agent Victor Graham."

"Already? Outstanding."

"Well, actually, sir, as it turns out, we don't exactly need to surveil him."

"What do you mean, Reynolds?"

"Well, you see, he's dead, sir."

"What?!"

"The police just found his body in the Thames. He'd been shot. Execution style, sir. In the back of the head."

**20**

**—·—**

The preliminary police report showed nothing beyond the initial news: MI5 agent Victor Graham was killed by a bullet to the back of the head and dumped into the river. No witnesses, no leads.

The last anyone had seen of Graham was at MI5 headquarters at Thames House the night before. Naturally, his task force was working around the clock, but in the evening, he had stepped out alone for a bite to eat. He told no one where he was going, but said he'd be back in an hour. He never returned.

"I know where he went," said Kori. "He went to the Connaught to have a drink with me. I told him about John Holland really being John Turner."

Kori and Anya were still in Chief Security Officer Bentley Hayes's office at MI6 headquarters. Hayes had placed a call to MI5 to ascertain the details, such as were known, of the murder of Graham.

"They must have grabbed him after he left the hotel," said Anya.

"And shot him and dumped him," Hayes added.

"Well, if that doesn't prove Graham was involved, I don't know what does," said Kori. "Cripes, they were probably afraid of what he was telling me. Of course, he hadn't told me anything, but they didn't know that. I mean, that explains why he was so reluctant to meet with me and share information. The mob was watching him and he knew it. He didn't tell them we had checked out of the Savoy and gone to the Connaught, Anya. They found out by following him."

"It might have been the same goons that you ran into this morning," Anya said.

"Geez, you're right. That's a sobering thought. If my man Fletch hadn't come along, they might have been fishing two bodies out of the Thames."

"Which begs another question," said Hayes. "I don't necessarily disagree that it's a mob killing, same as the execution of Burke. But it's not really a mob trait to allow their victims' bodies to be found so easily. If the London mafia has it in for you, you're likely to never be found. These discoveries in the Thames—a tad sloppy, no?"

"Maybe to throw us off the scent?" Anya offered.

"Agreed," said Kori. "Maybe they don't want to *look* like the London mafia. They don't want to give themselves away so they're intentionally sloppy. Plus, there's another purpose served. Maybe they're trying to make a statement. They want us to know they're serious. After all, let's not forget that the queen is on record as saying she won't pay the ransom. It could be that they're hoping these killings change her mind."

"Very possible," said Hayes. "Either way, the next step is clear. We have more than enough at this point to bring John Holland in for questioning."

"My thoughts exactly," said Kori.

"Now, this is the proper jurisdiction of MI5. Obviously, they're in a bit of turmoil right now, given that the head of the task force has been murdered. But let me make a call over there. I want you two to head to MI5 forthwith. I will set you up with whoever is now in command and I want you to tell them everything you've told me. Don't skip any details. We'll have Holland brought in and I will insist that you two be present for the questioning."

"We can't thank you enough," said Kori.

"It is we who should be thanking you," said Hayes. "Now, finally, maybe we can make some progress. Do you know where MI5 headquarters is?"

"Of course," replied Kori. "Just across the bridge."

"Very good. I'll make sure that you'll be expected by the time you get there."

"How is the bump on the head?" Anya asked.

"Still there," Kori replied. "Overall, it's giving me a dull headache. Then again, so is the case, so what's the difference?"

Thames House was a mere twelve-minute walk from the SIS building. Figuring it would take that long just to find a parking spot, the agents decided to leave their car in the care of MI6 and hoof it. The route took them back across the Thames over the Vauxhall Bridge and then along a pedestrian river walk for a couple of blocks. To the left of the agents, traffic buzzed along Millbank, the street that ran beside the river walk; to their right were the brown waters of the Thames, barges and tour boats navigating the river.

"But now we are getting somewhere," said Anya.

"Exactly. We're at least able to participate, although now it's clear why Graham was so reticent."

"So how do you think he was involved, Kori?"

"Well, of course, there's no telling how much he purposely hampered the investigation, not just ours, but MI5's. We may never know. The way I see it, Graham was either on the mob's payroll or he was being blackmailed to stymie the process. Maybe the mob had something on him."

"That makes sense. But I wonder—"

Anya wouldn't be able to finish the thought. Kori saw it first out of the corner of her eye, but by the time the van jumped the curb and slammed to a halt in front of them, it was too late to do much of anything. The agents stopped in their tracks and assumed defensive stances but six large men had the element of surprise and remarkable speed on their side. They jumped from the back of the van, grabbed Kori and Anya, and whisked them inside in seconds. As her hands were being bound behind her and a pillowcase pulled over her head, Kori knew that this was not an amateur operation. This was the London mafia.

"Funny, I don't remember calling for a cab," Kori said. "But as long as you're here, you mind giving us a lift to Jean-Georges at the Connaught? I could use some lunch. Anya, you hungry?"

"Famished," came Anya's reply from the darkness.

"Shut up," a stern voice commanded and then Kori felt the blow of an elbow to her forehead.

"Hey, was that really necessary?"

"Say one more word and you'll get much worse."

*Good time to be quiet*, Kori thought. "Much worse" was what she was suddenly expecting. On her knees on the floor of the van, hands secured behind her back with a zip tie, vision obscured by the pillowcase, she wondered if this was how Burke was handled. And Graham. Were they walking along and then abruptly shoved into a van? And were they shot in the van or were they shot elsewhere? *Most likely elsewhere*, Kori thought. *Too much of a mess in the van.* They were probably driven to some remote place, executed, then placed back in the van to be dropped into the river. However it was done, Kori had the uneasy feeling that she and Anya were next in line.

Kori tried to keep her bearings as the van drove along, but it made several turns over the course of the next twenty minutes before finally rolling to a stop. Kori could hear the rear doors of the van open and then felt herself being unceremoniously pushed out onto pavement. A grunt from Anya told her that she had landed right beside her. Kori then felt the rough hands of two men grabbing each of her arms, picking her up, and hustling her forward. A door opened and she sensed she was now being led inside a building. *Hmm, figured we'd be offed in a wooded area somewhere. Of course, the building might be soundproof. No one will hear the shots.*

After twenty or so steps, Kori was pressed into a chair. Someone yanked off the pillowcase and she could see that Anya was seated in the chair next to her, the pillowcase having been removed from her head, too. Both agents sat across a metal desk from a compact, muscular man with slicked-back hair wearing a dark, slim-fit suit. Up close, Kori could see that Andrew Quincy was probably older than she had thought. His weathered face made him look to be in his forties, not his thirties, and his crooked nose betrayed the fights he'd obviously been in. This guy was mob muscle in the flesh.

"So what can we do for you, sporty?" Kori asked.

Quincy leaned back in his chair, studying both women. Kori glanced about the cramped office. There was a calendar whiteboard with markings on certain days—probably days of incoming shipments, posters of MMA fighters and lingerie models on the walls, a laptop and a half-eaten sandwich on the desk, and a shelf with sample merchandise identical to what Kori and Anya had found in the warehouse in Rothton. In fact, Kori surmised that's where they were. This was Quincy's office at the front of the Hudson Imports warehouse building.

"You can start by telling me who you are," Quincy said.

"I'm Miss Marple and this is my associate, Miss Silver."

Two of the goons from the van had remained in Quincy's office. Quincy nodded to one of them and he strode toward Kori and slapped her hard across the face.

"Sorry," Kori said, shaking her head to flick her hair back in place. "I meant to say that I'm Miss Silver and *she's* Miss Marple."

This time, the goon didn't need the nod. He slapped her again.

"What is it with you guys?" Kori said. "Didn't your fathers ever teach you not to hit women?"

"I'll ask once more, and then we'll do much more than hit you, I assure you."

Kori said nothing for a moment and then decided it might not be the worst thing in the world to at least offer their names. She glanced over at Anya who shrugged in apparent agreement. "I'm Briggs and this is Kovalev," Kori said at last.

"I know *that*," Quincy said impatiently. "We're not stupid. I mean who *are* you? Who are you with? What are you doing here?"

So that's why they were sitting in the warehouse building. And that's why they were still alive. Quincy was probably going to kill them, but he needed to first know what they knew and who they were in contact with.

Evidently, they were still a mystery to him. That gave her and Anya a slight edge, or at least some temporary hope.

Kori thought quickly. *How much to tell?* What could she say that wouldn't give too much away while keeping them both alive? Quincy no doubt knew about them through Victor Graham. But he didn't know they were with Rampart because Graham didn't even know they were with Rampart. Graham had figured CIA. Maybe she could use that. Rampart wouldn't mean anything to Quincy, but the CIA surely would.

"We're with the US Central Intelligence Agency," she replied. "Maybe you've heard of us."

Anya picked it up from there. "The agency also knows we were on our way to meet with MI5," she said. "They will wonder where we are."

"And they will come looking for us," added Kori.

"Well, I wouldn't worry about that," said Quincy with a smirk. "I don't think they'll find you here."

Quincy apparently didn't realize that Kori and Anya knew about Hudson Imports. She'd mentioned it to Graham, but he must not have passed that along to the mob. Of course not. Graham understood that if the mob knew the agents were learning too much, they'd have him killed. That is, in fact, what had happened. It stood to reason that he hadn't told them they knew about John Holland, either. If Quincy thought the agents knew about Holland, they'd certainly end up in the Thames. Kori figured that's why Quincy must have had them brought to the warehouse—to find out if they knew that Sir John

Holland, philanthropist and billionaire, was really John Turner, head of London's organized crime.

"Now tell me why you're here," Quincy said. "What are two CIA agents doing in London?"

"We were invited to have tea with the queen," Kori replied. The goon took a step toward her, raising his hand. "Okay, okay. We're investigating Prince Grayson's disappearance. What else would we be doing?" The goon stepped back. "Now, if I could be permitted a question, who exactly are you?"

"As if you don't know," Quincy said. Kori and Anya looked at each other and shrugged. Quincy's brow furrowed. Kori could tell he was now wondering if it was possible that they *didn't* know who he was. Maybe they knew nothing about the mob, in which case Quincy had misplayed his cards by bringing them in. Certainly, he couldn't have them killed now. Two dead CIA agents would be bad for business. But he couldn't take them back, either. They were going to wonder who had nabbed them and why. Investigations would follow. Quincy had put himself into a quandary and Kori was beginning to realize that Turner must not have hired him for his brains. On the other hand, Turner had to have known that Kori and Anya were hot on the trail. Maybe the idea was to keep them bottled up, relegate them to the sidelines. He didn't need to have them killed; he just needed to take them out of the game.

Quincy's next line confirmed it. "Take them to the dungeon, boys. Lock 'em up."

## 21

— · —

From a theatrical point of view, the dungeon was a bit of a disappointment. It was not a medieval castle basement with cold, stone walls, torch lights, chains, and torture devices. It was another office in the same building with its windows blacked out, two folding chairs on a concrete floor, and little else. "The dungeon" was clearly a pet name.

The goons shoved the agents into the chairs, turned, and walked out of the office, locking the door behind them. Kori and Anya were free to move about the room, but their hands were still zip-tied behind their backs.

"Blood," Anya said quietly, nodding her head toward the floor in front of them. The floor was stained with it.

"Graham's, I'll bet," said Kori. "They probably beat him before they shot him, trying to determine what he had passed along to us."

"They will beat us and kill us, too."

"Maybe. But maybe not. We're CIA, at least in their minds. That makes it a different ballgame. They know that if we turn up dead or missing, US government agents will be all over London. Don't get me wrong; Graham's murder will be investigated, too. But something tells me the investigation will close quickly."

"Why?"

"Because of Graham's involvement with the mob. In the course of investigating his death, the police will investigate Graham himself—his contacts, his bank accounts, his recent movements, everything. They'll discover his moonlighting for Turner."

"Assuming he was moonlighting voluntarily. Like you said, Kori, maybe he was being blackmailed by the mob. Maybe they had something on him."

"But that something would still be bad. Either way, he was tied to the mob and that would be bad publicity for MI5."

"I see what you mean."

"If they find his murderer, probably Quincy himself, then the murderer will squeal about Graham's involvement. Will the public think that MI5 is tainted? The person who was appointed head of the task force to find Prince Grayson turned out to have mob ties? Trust me, any investigation of Graham's death is going to end almost before it begins. They'll say he was on a stakeout that went bad or something. No matter how he was killed, it's not a good look for the agency in the middle of the Grayson case. I'll bet they're already concocting some story. They'll want to keep Graham's death out of the press as long as they can."

"And release the details only after the case is resolved."

"Sure."

"So why do you think the mob killed him?"

"I'm sure his job was to purposely slow down the investigation, right? And concerning us, to throw us off track. But although he tried, he wasn't doing an effective enough job. Quincy was following us with his boys out there. He watched me pay visits to Kingsley and Bates. Twice with Bates, in fact. He saw us go to White's. He probably didn't see us sneak into Grayson's manor, and I'm sure he didn't follow us to Cambridge."

"How do you know?"

"We'd be dead. He'd know we were making the Holland–Turner connection. But still, he saw enough of our investigation to believe that Graham was telling us things, even though he wasn't. Quincy was afraid we were getting too close to the truth. I'm sure Graham swore up and down that he'd kept his mouth shut as he sat right here being questioned and beaten."

"Evidently, they did not care for his answers."

"Nope."

"As for us, I agree that they cannot kill us, but neither can they let us go, Kori."

"Yeah, looks like we're stuck right here for a while. My guess is that once this thing is over—the ransom is paid, or, failing that, Grayson is killed—then maybe they'll let us go. Put us back in the van, drive us out to the country somewhere, and drop us off like unwanted kittens. Hudson Imports will pack it up and open somewhere else under a new name. Quincy will lie low, maybe take an extended vacation until everything blows over. Turner's secret will remain a secret, or at least that's what they'll believe. They'll think they'll have left us with no clues and nothing to investigate."

"You are more of an optimist than I am, my friend. They may not kill us, but it is entirely possible we could be in for a good old-fashioned—how do you say?—ass-whupping, just to make sure we are telling the truth when we say we do not know anything."

Kori chuckled. "Maybe. A few bruises, perhaps a broken nose, a fat lip. Nothing that won't heal."

"Well, when you put it like that . . ."

"In the meantime, maybe we can find a way out of here."

"I am open to any and all ideas."

Kori and Anya paced around the office, looking for, well, looking for something they could use. Anything. Kori wondered if they could break a window. Maybe they could push a chair toward the window, step up on the chair, and dive through. She knew they were on the ground floor, after all. Anya wondered if they could somehow summon the goons, crouch behind the door, and knock them senseless when they entered. Both trains of thought were full of holes and neither would work very well with the agents' hands rendered immobile behind them.

Clearly, they were stuck.

Several minutes came and went with both agents lost in thought. Then suddenly they heard a commotion outside the building which carried into the front office. Kori and Anya heard voices and shots fired. More shots followed. Then more voices.

Then quiet.

Finally, the agents heard a voice outside the door. "They must be in here, mates." The door knob turned slightly. "Locked, of course. Agents Briggs and Kovalev, are you in there?"

"Yes," Kori said.

"Stand aside from the door, if you please."

A moment later, the door crashed open. A man in tactical gear with an entry ram, followed by two others, barreled into the room.

"Good day, agents," the man with the ram said. "My name is Walsh. We're MI6."

"Good to see you, Walsh," Kori replied. "Needless to say."

One of the other MI6 men took out a knife and cut through the zip ties.

"How did you know where we were?" Anya asked, rubbing her wrists.

"Chief Hayes had a man follow you from his office," Walsh said.

"Wow, what a guy," said Kori.

"Yes, Chief Hayes always seems to have a sense about these things. He wanted to take no chances."

"We have a chief like that ourselves."

"Sorry we didn't get here sooner. Our man notified us you were snatched and we responded as fast as we could. We lost your van, but our helo picked it up again and led us here."

"Where are Quincy and the others?"

"The blokes that kidnapped you? We traded a few shots with them and then they scurried out the back. Bastards had a speedboat tied up to the dock. Can you believe it?"

"So they got away."

"Afraid so. But our helo is still in the air. We'll find 'em."

"Anybody get hurt?"

"No, I believe we're all in splendid shape. But now, Ms. Briggs and Ms. Kovalev, if you'll please come with us. Chief Hayes has informed us that you're late for a meeting at Thames House with the MI5 task force, a meeting he himself arranged."

"I'm afraid we are at that," said Kori.

"Well, then. We'll give you a lift. You can make your apologies when you get there."

The meeting with the task force at Thames House was less productive than Kori had hoped. She and Anya hadn't learned much more than they'd already known. For their part, MI5 appreciated the Holland–Turner connection and everyone seemed to agree that the connection extended, in some way, to the prince's disappearance. But Chief Hayes had been overly optimistic. The circumstantial nature of the link meant that Sir John

Holland could be asked to come in for questioning, but he could not be forced to.

Certainly, Andrew Quincy could be arrested and, in fact, the issuance of a warrant was underway. Unfortunately, it had come to light during the meeting that the pilot of the helicopter monitoring the speedboat observed the boat come ashore in a wooded area in East Tilbury, then lost the crew in the trees. Police converged on the area, but Quincy and his men were nowhere to be found. Undoubtedly, Quincy had called other mob members for help. The wooded area was probably a prearranged meeting spot; a car and driver had most likely been waiting for them on the other side of the trees where there was a busy street, picking them up and blending into traffic. Now there was no telling where Quincy was.

The agents further learned that Newton Dempsey had been in contact with Buckingham Palace twice since his original email, both times more or less demanding updates. Just that morning, he had sent an email to remind the queen, as if she needed a reminder, that the following day would be "the prince's last on this earth if the money does not make it into the account." The queen had remained adamant, reminding the prime minister, who had passed her sentiments along to MI5, that "We have never, and will not now, negotiate with kidnappers or terrorists. The fact that the life of a royal is at stake, painful as it might be for your queen on a personal level, does not alter this doctrine." Nevertheless, word out of the palace was that the queen's condition had been elevated from "concerned" to "quite agitated" by the lack of progress being made on Prince Grayson's rescue.

There was one positive, perhaps helpful, thing that the Rampart agents learned. Newton Dempsey had been spotted two days before. Someone had recognized him in a supermarket in St. John's Wood. His picture as a person of interest had made the rounds on TV and social media, and some observant shopper had seen him in a checkout lane. He had a mustache, but she was sure it was him and called the police. In truth, it was one of hundreds of reported sightings of Dempsey. The public still didn't know the scope or nature of his involvement, as Buckingham Palace had insisted that no news of a kidnapping be reported, but that didn't stop the leads from coming in. None of them, besides this one, had panned out. MI5 had taken store video footage, enhanced it, run it through a facial recognition program, and determined that the man in the checkout lane was, indeed, Newton Dempsey with a false mustache. Consequently, it was believed that wherever he was holding the prince, it was most likely not far from the store. No doubt he was there to restock food and other miscellaneous staples. Where he went from the store, no one could say, but roads in and out of the area were now patrolled by the police, and cars were routinely stopped and checked. But Dempsey's appearance was not relayed to the media; MI5 did not want Dempsey to know he'd been spotted.

And that was the gist of the briefing. Of course, the entire agency was reeling from the death of Victor Graham and his possible connection to the London mafia, but that matter would have to wait. The deadline was fast approaching. And Kori had been right; news of Graham's murder was being temporarily withheld from the press.

Kori and Anya had been brought up to speed but were left with little direction. After thanking their counterparts and being promised that they'd be privy to the latest information, they left MI5 headquarters. Instead of walking this time, they hailed a cab. "Quincy and his cohorts know our car," Kori said. "Let's leave it where we parked it."

With nowhere else to go and the day getting late, Kori suggested they check out the supermarket where Dempsey was last seen. "I can't imagine we're going to find anything that the police didn't find," Kori said, "but I guess you never know. Can you think of anything else?"

"I'm afraid not," Anya replied. "And I fear time is running out on the prince. Tomorrow is just a few hours away. But we will figure it out, Kori. We always do."

Kori nodded as the two stepped into a cab and headed to the supermarket in St. John's Wood. But Anya knew enough about her partner to know this: Kori was unconvinced.

# 22

—·—

The store manager had been on duty when Newton Dempsey had made his appearance but said she hadn't personally seen him. She'd been in the back office at the time. The manager was able to show Kori and Anya a copy of Dempsey's receipt, but the agents had already seen it at MI5 headquarters. Eggs, bread, ground beef, some frozen foods, assorted fruits, cereal, milk—it could have been the grocery list of anybody in the world.

"Might I ask who this fellow is?" the manager said. "Everybody certainly is making quite the fuss over him."

"Oh, nobody, really," Kori replied. "We just think he might know something that can help us. Got to follow every lead, right?"

"Well, I hope you find him. It's just an awful thing, the prince missing. Can't remember anything like this happening before. Just awful."

"Indeed it is. Well, thank you for your time."

"Of course. Happy to help any way I can, I'm sure."

The agents stepped back outside.

"What now?" Anya asked.

Kori sighed and looked off into the distance, mulling things over. *What now indeed?* Then she happened to glance to her right and something caught her eyes between the trees across the street.

"Anya," she said. "The row of large houses beyond that grove of trees. You see them?"

"Sure. Well, I mean I can see their rooftops.

"The second one on the left. That chimney looks damn familiar, doesn't it? The odd shape, the red brick."

Anya squinted. "Classic Victorian chimney stack. Dual pots."

"Dual what?"

"The two red clay extensions at the top. You are observant, my friend. I believe that is indeed the place you are thinking of."

Kori checked the map on her phone.

"That's it all right," she said. "It's funny, but I wasn't really paying attention to just where we were as we were riding in the cab. I mean, I knew we were headed to St. John's Wood, but did you realize we were this close to the prince's manor?"

"No idea. Does it mean anything?"

"I don't know. Maybe not. I mean, MI5 didn't say anything about it. I suppose it only stands to reason that Dempsey and the late Spencer Burke wouldn't want to travel too far with the prince." Kori became quiet and thoughtful for a moment.

"Ah, I can tell that the wheels are turning, are they not? Anya asked. "Do you want to share what you are thinking?"

"Well, Anya, it's probably nothing, but think about this: What if Dempsey and Burke and Grayson didn't travel anywhere at all? A couple of things have been sort of popping up in my head that I can't seem to shake. For instance, do you remember the Stewarts talking about the secret passageway?"

"Of course."

"They said the only other person who knew about it was the prince. And something else: why was there no mention in the crime scene report about the imprints of the presumed ladder that was used in the kidnapping? Graham talked about the ladder, but only after I asked about it. And I haven't seen anything more about it. Now, I figured that maybe Graham just gave me a partial file and that little piece of information was left out, among other things. But what if it was never in there? What if a ladder was never even used? What if the prince wasn't taken out the window?"

"You think they took the prince out through the passageway?"

"Maybe. Either that or they never took him out at all. It's a big house, Anya."

"You think he's hidden away like the Stewarts were?"

"We've seen stranger things, no?"

"I suppose it is possible."

"And another thing. What was Quincy doing at the manor anyway? What was behind the two visits?"

"I assumed he was threatening the prince. To shake him down for the money he owed Turner."

"I assumed that, too. But maybe it was to hatch the kidnapping plot."

Anya's eyes got big. "Kori, you think the prince was *in* on it?!"

"Well, no, I mean, not voluntarily. But if the prince didn't have the money, then wouldn't Turner naturally consider Grayson's family money? The royal money? So maybe Quincy threatened Grayson, but not to pay his debts, which he couldn't do anyway, but to go along with the kidnapping plot. To even help in its execution. And when the London mafia asks you to go along with something, you go along with it."

"That explains the disabled alarm more than anything else."

"Exactly!"

"The prince became an involuntary accomplice. But it was the only way he could pay his debt. There is an old Russian proverb, Kori. 'When you owe someone a little, you have a creditor. When you owe someone a lot, you have a partner.'"

"Royalty and mafia. Interesting partnership."

"So I presume you will want to pay another visit to the prince's manor?"

"Well, as long as we're this close, right?"

This time, the agents used the passageway, although Kori reflected on how much more fun it was to climb the trellis.

"Fun for you maybe," said Anya.

Once they accessed the ballroom, they took a very slow walk around the first floor, inspecting each room but finding nothing amiss and no sign that the prince was hidden away in his own home. They walked stealthily, Anya leading the way holding her Sig Sauer ahead of her. Kori desperately missed her Glock.

They walked around the second floor as well, through the servant's quarters and spare bedrooms. Finding nothing, they finally patrolled the third, checking out the breakfast room, media room, library, and eventually, stopping off in the prince's master suite.

The agents looked around, seeing nothing out of the ordinary. Anya poked her head into the large bathroom while Kori sauntered into the dressing area. She looked once again at the long rack of clothes and the shelves of shoes. But this time, she noticed something different. The Brunello Cucinelli sweatsuit was missing. So was the Landon lambskin bomber jacket.

She retreated to the bedroom and whispered to Anya, "The prince has been here."

"How do you know?"

"Some of his clothes are missing. Now, either he was here or someone decided to come and pick up a few things on his behalf."

"Nobody is here now, Kori. We have searched high and low."

"We've only searched the areas of the house that are apparent."

"You are suggesting hidden places."

"Sure. These big old mansions always have little hidden places. Some designed during construction, some added later. False walls, secret panels, all kinds of ways to conceal someone. Heck, there's probably a panic room somewhere, too, for security."

"Hmm . . . perhaps."

"The problem is finding it."

"That is not so much a problem, Kori."

"No? What do you suggest?"

"Simple. Infrared imaging."

"Of course! We can search for body heat. But where are we going to get an infrared camera? It has to be a good one, too. Most commercial models won't pick up much through walls. We need a military-grade model."

"Surely MI6 has them."

"Another good idea. When this is over, make sure to take a little something extra for yourself out of petty cash. Come on, let's get out of here. We'll call Chief Hayes."

Chief Security Officer Bentley Hayes listened intently to Kori's thoughts on the possible whereabouts of the prince and, within an hour, an MI6 drone equipped with a high-grade, ultra-max, forward-looking infrared camera was dispatched to the manor, buzzing all around it for a solid half hour while the agents watched from across the street. A few members of the ever-present paparazzi were still hanging about the house, but if they noticed the drone at all in the dark, they thought little of it. At four feet across, it was probably bigger than what anybody might have seen around the prince's mansion, but it certainly wasn't the first drone that had circled the property. Some had belonged to law enforcement; some had been sent from the paparazzi; quite illegally, but impossible to catch.

Finally, Kori's phone buzzed. "Yes, Chief Hayes?" she answered.

"We're watching it from the screen here, Agent Briggs. We've been all around the property. Sorry to say that nothing is showing up. There's not a single warm body in that house."

"Damn. Sorry, Chief. False alarm, I guess."

"No worries, Agent Briggs. It was an ace idea, if you ask me, and well worth trying, if for no other reason than to eliminate the possibility. I'm sorry it didn't pan out. Well, do keep in touch, won't you?"

"Of course, and thank you again, Chief Hayes." Kori hung up and she and Anya watched as the drone made its way back to MI6, disappearing against the night sky. "Well, that was certainly disappointing."

"Yes, it was. I had convinced myself we would find them."

"Me too."

The agents sat across from the house in silence for a few minutes. Finally, because somebody had to, Anya asked the obvious. "What now?"

Kori sighed. "Well, I don't guess there's anything more we can do tonight. Tomorrow's the deadline but, you know, I have a feeling Buckingham Palace will be hearing from Dempsey before then. Turner's going to want to give the queen one last chance, right?"

"I would think so. Killing the prince means giving up any chance, no matter how small, for a lot of money."

"Right. So I guess all we can do now is sit tight and wait to hear from MI5."

"Where should we pass the night, Kori? It is not safe for us to go back to the Connaught."

"Agreed."

"Another hotel, close by?"

Kori gazed at the manor house in front of them. "Well, it seems a shame to spend Rampart's money on a hotel room when we have such lovely accommodations right here, doesn't it?"

Anya smiled. "It *is* a rather charming place. And I am always in favor of saving the agency a dollar when we can."

"Do you remember where that bar was on the first floor?"

"I'm sure we can find it. To the passageway?"

"To the passageway."

The best thing about the prince's bar was that the liquor was all top-shelf. Kori had a Scotch, Anya had a vodka, and they shared the beer nuts they managed to find.

At one point, Kori turned to her fellow agent and said, "Anya, how much of Prince Grayson's personal life do you suppose the queen knows?"

"You mean like his possible gambling addiction and his debts?"

"Yes."

"Who can say? She is a smart woman."

"I was thinking about those promissory notes and the purpose of them. Property of the royal family is tax exempt, you know."

"Yes, I had assumed so."

"It's held in a trust. But that means debts as well as assets."

"Meaning what exactly?"

"Meaning that if something should happen to good Prince Grayson, the royal family would be on the hook for his debts."

"If the debts are in writing," Anya nodded.

"Hence, the notes to JEH Financial."

"Yes, of course. Well, that explains that. Turner can simply collect from the royal family . . . So wait, Kori, are you thinking that Turner is going to have Grayson killed anyway?"

"I don't know. Maybe. In some sense, it would be a lot cleaner. Collecting ransoms are never easy."

"But then why go to the trouble of kidnapping him in the first place?"

"Looking for a bigger payday, I guess. Even for a billionaire, one hundred million dollars is a lot of money. But failing that, he can still go after the estate. Because of the existence of the promissory—"

"*Shhh . . .*" Anya said suddenly, reaching toward the wall and flicking off the light switch. Soon, Kori heard it, too. Footsteps upstairs.

"Cripes," she whispered, setting down her Scotch, "doesn't anybody respect the sanctity of a crime scene?"

**23**

—·—

Once again, Anya pulled out her gun and led the way; first up the stairs and then all around the second floor. They found nothing, but then heard the footsteps again above them.

"They've gone up a floor," Anya whispered.

"Yes, and that's the prince's bedroom above us," Kori said.

"Perhaps the prince came back."

"Let's go."

The two moved softly down the hall, up the stairs, through the anteroom of the master suite, and then ever so quietly into the master bedroom. Silhouetted against the wall was the figure of a man, a flashlight in his hand that was presently illuminating the bed in front of him.

"Freeze!" Anya called out.

Kori trained her phone's flashlight on the man's bewildered face, noticing something in his other hand. "Drop it!" she ordered.

The man dropped his flashlight and an object that was, upon closer inspection, a Sony digital camera. Kori swooped in and picked it up. The man tried to say something but was too startled to form words.

"Into the anteroom," Anya said, pointing the way. "Through there."

The man, tall and thin with straggly black hair, raised his hands and moved into the anteroom as Anya and Kori followed. Kori closed the bedroom door behind them and flipped on the light switch. "Have a seat," she said, shoving the man into a stuffed chair. Anya kept the gun on him.

The man finally managed to speak. "Who are you?"

"Squatters," said Kori. "We're thinking of living here. It's comfortable and convenient to work. That's our story, what's yours?"

"My name is Cameron Riley. But, look, I wasn't doing anything—"

"Aha! The one and only Cameron Riley of *Star Globe Magazine*?"

"Yes."

"We should have known. That explains the camera. Nice one, too. What did this sucker set you back?"

"I don't remember."

"I'll have to bust it up, of course. Sorry." Then Kori shook her head. "Cameron Riley. How about that? You're practically a celebrity yourself, you know. My mom's a big fan of yours."

Riley tried to smile.

"But I'm not."

Riley stopped trying to smile.

"So I guess we don't have to ask what you're doing here," Kori continued. "Getting pictures of the prince's bed.

That could sell a lot of papers and get a lot of clicks. What other pictures have you taken? Well, it doesn't matter. Nobody's going to see them anyway. How did you get in?"

"Through a second-floor window. I climbed up a trellis."

"Very resourceful."

"Yeah but, look, I'm not responsible for the hole in the window. That was already there."

Kori and Anya exchanged glances.

Riley went on the offensive. "So who are *you*, anyway? You sound American. Who are you with?"

There was no reason not to tell him unless he was wired or had a recording device on him.

"Stand up and put your hands against the wall," Kori ordered. "Then maybe I'll tell you." She frisked him, then spun him around and unbuttoned his shirt to check for a wire. "Don't get excited," she said. "You're not really my type." Riley was clean. Kori pushed him back into the chair.

"We're intelligence agents from the US here to investigate the prince's disappearance," said Kori. "And if you print a word of that, we'll deny it and then shut your rag down. You're in a whole hell of a lot of trouble, breaking in here. I'm going to have to call the police, you know."

"Come on, I was just trying to get a good scoop," Riley protested. "You can't blame a fella for that, now can you? The people want to stay informed."

"I see. And so you're only doing your duty to the people, is that it?"

"Well, sure."

"Anya, did you hear? This man is a hero."

"Okay, okay, I didn't say I was a hero. Still, there's no reason to have me arrested. I wasn't robbing the place or anything. Listen, maybe I can help you with your investigation. I might know some things. In return, you forget all about seeing me here. And I won't come back, I swear it."

Kori knew it was a desperate attempt by Riley, but then again, hadn't he indirectly tipped her off about the gambling debts? It's possible he might know something, and any scrap of information was welcome at this point. Besides, Kori knew they weren't really going to call the police. What would they say? That they caught somebody breaking into the prince's house after *they* had broken into the prince's house?

"Okay, scooter. We'll listen, but your information better be good."

"Well, what would you like to know?"

"How about the location of the prince?"

"Okay, so I don't exactly know that."

"Really? Your latest dispatch said he was spotted in Helsinki."

Riley chuckled. "Well, I mean, he could have been, right? Listen, ours is a highly competitive business. Sometimes you have to . . . embellish a little."

"Uh-huh. And he has a girlfriend, too, apparently. A twenty-two-year-old club dancer."

"Okay, a little more embellishment. But he does have a girlfriend."

"Really?"

"Yes. She's not twenty-two, nor is she a club dancer. She *is* younger, though; mid-thirties. And he is keeping the relationship a secret."

"Who is she?" Anya asked.

"I can't say."

"Can't or won't?" said Kori.

"I won't. I'm sorry. You see, we got wind of the romance, followed the prince around, and took some photos of him and his new girlfriend. With the very camera you just confiscated, as a matter of fact. Anyway, before we could publish the photos, my boss suddenly decided to kill the story."

"How come?"

"I don't know. I really don't. I was quite upset it about, actually."

"Pressure from the prince?"

"Maybe. But that's never stopped us before. The bottom line is, I was to swear I wouldn't reveal her name. My boss would sack me if he knew I told anyone about her. That's how serious he is about keeping a lid on the story."

"Okay," Kori said, pulling out her phone, "well, then, I guess we'll just have to call the police,"

"Okay, okay, wait!" Riley said. Kori put her phone down. "I can't tell you, but . . . if you just happened, let's say, to glance through the memory card of my camera, it's entirely possible that you might just find a picture of her. I'm sorry, that's the best I can do."

"All right, Riley. I guess that'll do. God forbid we'd be the cause of your unemployment. My mother would never forgive me. So how did you 'get wind' of this girlfriend anyway?"

"The way we get most of our leads. Someone tipped us off."

"Who?"

Riley sighed. "Again, you're going to be disappointed."

"You can't say."

"No. But not because of my boss. We took the tip on the condition that we wouldn't reveal the source. And I never reveal my confidential sources."

"A man of integrity, huh?"

"So where did the story of the twenty-two-year-old dancer come from?" asked Anya.

"Oh, well, we kind of liked the idea of the prince having a girlfriend. Figured a story like that would get some traction, you know? Since my boss wouldn't let us print anything on the real one, we more or less invented one."

"Do the police know about the real girlfriend?"

"The police? Ha! They never know anything."

Kori and Anya looked at each other, both wondering if there was anything more to be asked. Finally, Kori said, "So what else can you tell us, Riley?"

Riley looked thoughtful then shrugged.

"That's not a lot of information," Kori said. "A girlfriend whose name you can't reveal. But this is your lucky day. We have better things to do than deal with you. We'll escort you down to the second floor. Back down the trellis you go, and we'd better never see you within five miles of this place."

"What about my camera? I mean, you can take the memory card, but what about the camera?"

"Sorry, this baby stays. I've been thinking about taking up photography. Who knows, maybe I can work for the venerable *Star Globe* someday. A girl can dream, right?"

"Scroll through, look for the pictures of the woman with the prince, and see what you can find out, Coop." Kori and Anya had sent Riley down the trellis with yet one more warning about printing anything about their meeting, then gone downstairs to access Parker Bates's office. Anya had hacked into his computer and uploaded the contents of the memory card of Riley's camera to a Rampart server. "Not sure what you'll find," Kori continued, "but hopefully, it'll be something we can use."

"Will do," Cooper replied. "I'll get right back to you."

"Thanks." Kori hung up. "Nothing to do but wait, Anya."

"Perhaps we should wait in the bar," Anya suggested.

"Fine idea."

In the bar with a glass of Scotch in hand, Kori mused about Cameron Riley. "You know, if he had broken in an hour earlier, he'd have been spotted by the drone."

"This really is his lucky day," Anya said. "So why do you think his boss killed the story of the real girlfriend?"

"I imagine someone approached him and offered to buy him off, don't you?"

"I suppose. But who? The prince himself?"

"I guess. Maybe we'll know more when we learn the identity of the girlfriend."

"Yes. In the meantime, I wonder what Cameron Riley will write about next. He might write about us, Kori."

"Possibly. He probably saw the blood on the bed, too. I told him we'd shut his paper down if he reported about us or anything he saw tonight, but he must know we can't really do that. There's no telling what kind of story he'll concoct. Or how much truth there will be to it. Of course, I'll hear all about it from my mom."

"I am sure you will."

"So, are there gossip rags in Russia?"

"Ha! All the news in Russia is gossip. Of course, it is presented by the state-controlled media outlets as fact. The constitution speaks of freedom of the press, but censorship is rampant. The human rights organization Freedom House has listed Russia at number 176 out of 197 for press freedom, slightly above Ethiopia and Sudan."

"Not very good."

"Nope."

"So, listen, why do you think nobody we've talked to has mentioned Prince Grayson's girlfriend?"

"Maybe they do not know."

"I find that hard to believe. Parker Bates, Kingsley Moore, the Stewarts—these people see him every day. At all hours. They're as close as family, probably closer than Grayson's real family. Moore and the Stewarts live here, for crying out loud, under the same roof."

"Then they are complicit in his keeping the relationship a secret."

"Yeah, but somebody blabbed. Someone leaked the relationship to the *Star Globe*. I wonder who, and I wonder why."

"The 'why' is easy. For money."

"Yes, I suppose. Someone called the *Star Globe* offering a juicy piece of information in exchange for a nice-sized check. And now that I think about it, I think I know who."

"Who?"

"The couple who couldn't afford to leave here, Anya. The couple who couldn't afford a hotel room."

"The Stewarts!"

"Makes sense, doesn't it? 'Hotels are so expensive,' Charles had said. They even talked about how they couldn't afford a new TV."

"Kori, I think you might be right."

"I knew it. I knew the butler did it! We just didn't know what he did. Well, now we know. He sold some gossip to a trash magazine. I suppose that's not a crime."

"Hmm . . . perhaps it ought to be."

"Censorship? Hey, don't go all Russian on me."

They both laughed and then Kori's phone rang: Cooper. Kori put the phone on speaker.

"What's the skinny, Coop?"

"The girlfriend's name is Felicity Watts, Kori."

"Never heard of her."

"I hadn't either. I ran facial recognition and that's the name that came up."

"What did you find on her?"

"Well, she has an interesting backstory. First of all, she's recently divorced. Watts is her married name. Care to guess what her maiden name is?"

"Tell me."

"Holland."

"Holland?!"

"She's John Holland's daughter."

"No way!"

"One and the same."

"So Prince Grayson is dating John Holland's daughter?"

"That's sure what it seems like. Your man Riley had taken pictures of them out for a walk somewhere. A park, it looks like. Maybe Hampstead Heath, but I can't really tell for sure. Anyway, they're holding hands and everything."

"You got an address on Felicity Watts?"

"Sure. She's got an apartment that she only recently started renting: 12 Mereside Road. And only about two blocks from where you are. Guess she wanted to be closer to her boyfriend."

"Thanks, Coop, I owe you another beer."

"Don't worry, I'm keeping track."

Kori hung up and turned to Anya. "Anya, do you think the prince knows exactly who he's dating? The daughter of the head of the London mafia?"

"Doubtful. There is no reason to believe that he knows who Holland really is, so why would he know who Felicity really is?"

"I agree. Then he would have no reason to buy off the story. There's no shame in a prince dating the daughter of a respected billionaire."

"So maybe it was Holland who bribed the *Star Globe* to not run the story."

"Or threatened. Remember who we're dealing with."

"True. Holland—Turner—probably did not want the extra attention. He has spent his life trying to keep a low profile. But, Kori, where is this all getting us? How does this all connect to the kidnapping?"

"Yeah, I know, things still don't make a lot of sense. Of course, we do know one thing for sure. Newton Dempsey has been seen in this very neighborhood. We also know that they're not keeping the prince here. So there must be another location close by. One the prince might be familiar with."

"12 Mereside Road."

"Two blocks from here."

"So what are we waiting for?"

**24**

—·—

Andrew Quincy looked around the room in disgust. Amateurs, all of them. Well, maybe the American had some smarts. Newton Dempsey acted like a man with experience. Wasn't there something in his background about some big con he'd played? But it was still a mystery to Quincy why Dempsey was even involved. Most of the time, it seemed as if London was the last place in the world he wanted to be.

It was 2 a.m. The deadline was already here. This was the day.

Four men sat in a living room, lights low, shades drawn. Four stuffed chairs, one for each man and one for each corner of the room. The men sat equidistant from each other, ten feet apart, a round coffee table between them. Waiting. Quincy was the only one holding a gun, a Glock he'd recently come into possession of. A nice one, too.

Newton Dempsey sat in a chair nursing a drink, frequently checking his laptop. But Buckingham Palace was not responding.

John Holland, who had kept insisting that he be called nothing else, was idly flipping through a glamour magazine, not the choice of magazine he would have necessarily made under other circumstances, but his daughter's coffee table didn't offer much of a selection.

Across from Holland sat the man himself. Quincy was not impressed. Frankly, he'd been nothing but a pain in the ass, the old sod, requiring special food, forcing Quincy to go back to the manor to retrieve clothing, even demanding bottles of Foragers Clogau Reserve gin. One hundred and sixty quid a bottle! Good God, no wonder the man was in so much debt. As if Gordon's wasn't good enough.

Quincy was sick of all of them. And what a daft idea in the first place. No real surprise that Quincy was the one chosen to see it through. He seemed to get all the dirty work. How many years had he been working now for the boss? "You're the only one I trust with this," he'd told Quincy. Well, that was nice to hear, but what he really wanted to hear was that he was being promoted to a position where he wouldn't have to worry about sitting in a living room at two in the morning with a bunch of charlies like these blokes. When was that day going to come?

Maybe never. Quincy was too good at what he did. Maybe that was the problem. He was too good to be promoted. What did they call that? Ironic? Besides, he wasn't a Turner. He was a Quincy, just a ham-and-egger from Southwark. And a Quincy could never be a Turner. All he could do was put his head down and keep going, taking the assignments he was given, no matter how distasteful or daft, and hoping against hope that his loyalty would be rewarded.

Of course, the boss was going to reward him for this job, that was a certainty. Victor Graham had been Quincy's contact, after all. They'd known each other from primary school back in Southwark, but you'd never get Graham to admit he was from the streets just like Quincy. One went one way, one went the other. It was nice having a contact on the police force, especially one as high up as Graham. And one as willing to take bribes. Well, you know what they say; you can take the man out of Southwark, but you can't take Southwark out of the man. Damn shame that Quincy had to kill him, but he'd outlived his usefulness. He was doing fine bolloxing up MI5's investigation, but he was letting those two American birds get way too close. Who were they anyway? Who sent them? Good thing that he'd had Graham followed or he might never have known about them. They were elusive, whoever they were. But he'd find them.

He didn't especially like having to burn Spenser Burke, but Burke had outlived his usefulness, too. The boss thought he'd be more valuable as a statement showing how serious the kidnappers were and Quincy had agreed. Apparently, it was all for naught, though. Buckingham Palace didn't seem to care. What was with the old woman anyway? Was she really just going to let them whack her own son? How cold can you be?

John Holland looked up from his magazine. "What time is it now?" he asked.

"Ten minutes after the last time you asked," Quincy replied. "You'd think a nob like you would have a watch."

Holland ignored him. "Dempsey?" he said. "Still nothing? Email them again. Tell 'em we're serious this time."

"What do you think I've been telling them?" Dempsey said, raising his voice.

"Maybe they're all asleep."

Dempsey sighed. "For the hundredth time, it's the address of the Lord Chamberlain of the Royal Household. It's monitored twenty-four hours a day. Nobody's asleep. They're just choosing not to answer us. And who can blame them? I told you—I told all of you—this was the stupidest idea of all time. You think they're really going to hand over one hundred million dollars?"

Newton Dempsey looked around the room in disgust. Ten years in Rikers Island only to end up here? With these losers? He had the beginnings of a good life going back in Boston. Selling cars wasn't the most exciting thing in the world, but he still got a thrill out of talking someone into a car they didn't really need. Sure, it wasn't like conning people out of millions of dollars, but then again, it wasn't illegal, either. He'd be damned if he was ever going back to prison. He vowed that those days were behind him.

And then that damn Spenser Burke had shown up. Out of the blue. Over fish and chips at O'Shaughnessy's, he introduced himself. Turns out, his boss was John Holland. And John Holland was still pissed off. Ten years had come and gone, but guys like Holland don't forget it when you take twenty million dollars of their money.

Holland was the perfect example of someone too rich for his own good. Holland believed himself brilliant, thought of himself as the world's smartest businessman. But of course, that's what had made him such an easy mark. All you have to do with guys like Holland is play to their enormous egos. Holland had swallowed the "Next Great Thing" scam hook, line, and sinker. It was almost laughable the way that he couldn't bring himself to admit that he didn't understand the technology. Well, of course, he didn't. Nobody did. There wasn't anything to understand. It was all bullshit, but Holland's eyes lit up when he heard catch-phrases like, "Will revolutionize the internet," and, "The next generation of information technology." "We're going to make Google look like buggy whip manufacturers," Dempsey had promised. Holland didn't want to be left out.

Dempsey had told all the potential investors the same thing. "We're at a crossroads. Some will be a part of the future, feasting on the fruits of technology's next quantum leap; some will be left behind to scrounge for scraps through the decaying remnants of the past. Which do you want to be?" When he said this to John Holland, Holland had wired the twenty million the next day.

So anyway, there was Spenser Burke sipping on a Guinness at O'Shaughnessy's and explaining to Dempsey what would happen to him if he didn't fly back to London with him and help Holland execute this simple plan of his. Holland had been waiting cold and patiently for Dempsey to be released from Rikers. Dempsey might have paid his debt to society, but he hadn't paid his debt to Holland.

And, as it turned out, Holland knew some bad guys. Very bad guys. He'd given Burke a message to pass along: "You're at a crossroads, Newton. You can either play ball and have a future, or you can be dead." None too subtle, but clever in its own way.

Executing the plan would square the debt. The problem was that the simple plan wasn't so simple. It involved kidnapping a damn prince, for God's sake! Who does that? Who even *thinks* of doing that? "It'll go smoothly," Holland had promised. "The royal family will pay, you and I will be even, and I'll give you enough to get yourself back to Costa Rica with a new identity." It was either that or he'd be dead. And he knew that Holland and the bad guys who Holland knew were serious. This guy Quincy, for instance. Talk about playing hardball. Look at what happened to that MI5 detective. And Burke himself! Just to make a statement? Wow.

Truth be told, Dempsey couldn't figure out why Holland would let him live regardless of the outcome. Grayson's deadline might as well be his own. But maybe, just maybe, Holland would appreciate the way Dempsey had handled everything. He could only hope. What choice did he have? Of course, none of it would matter if Buckingham Palace didn't return his damn emails. "Today is the day," he had emailed at midnight. "If I don't see the money appear in the account, your prince will die."

Then, per the boss's instructions, he'd put a more specific deadline in place. "You have until 3 a.m." Surely that would force them to act. And now it was 2:30.

"Dempsey," Holland said through the silence that had enveloped them all, "when was the last time you checked the bank account?"

"Last Thursday," Dempsey replied, rolling his eyes. "When do you think? I'm checking it all the time! Every other minute!"

"I'm just asking."

"And I'm just telling. The goddamn account is just as empty now as it was the last time I checked."

The silence continued.

John Holland looked around the room in disgust. Dempsey was a sarcastic, two-bit hustler, but he might well have been right about one thing: This was the stupidest idea of all time. How did he allow himself to get talked into it? To team up with this roomful of snakes? For what? Friendship? Screw friendship. He'd spent his entire life trying to break away from his family, and his friendship with the prince had allowed them to drag him right back.

Holland hated his family. He hated the way they made their living. All through grade school, everyone knew who he was. It seems they sometimes knew more than he did. It started in first grade when a kid went up to him on the playground at recess and said, "I heard your father kills people." And it didn't get better from there.

Everyone in London knew the Turner name. It was so liberating to go away to university, the first time he'd ever been away from home. Nobody at Cambridge had any idea who he was and how his family had made their money. He felt normal for the first time in his life. He liked the feeling so much that he made it permanent, getting a false ID and changing his name at the school. Nobody could ever trace his new name to his old one unless they rummaged through the student records, and who would ever do that?

When he graduated, he returned to London with a beard and a nose job and lived as far away from his family as he could. The split hadn't exactly been welcomed by his father, but he had no choice other than to go along with it. Then Holland set about making his fortune. Over time, he shed the beard, leaving just a light mustache. Now, nobody knew where he'd come from. He made up a story about growing up in Canterbury and no one seemed especially interested in digging too deep; everyone wanted to know how he'd made his fortune and he was always happy to talk about his business acumen. The best part of the separation from the family was that he was judged on his own achievements, which were formidable.

Of course, every day he lived in fear that someone would make the connection, but at least he knew they wouldn't find out anything from the Turners themselves. The last thing they wanted was publicity. It was the only thing he shared with his natural family—a strong desire to keep a low profile.

Naturally, when Felicity was old enough, he felt obliged to tell her about her grandfather and uncle and the family. She had a right to know. But he'd made it clear that she also had an obligation to keep the secret. And she had. Her first husband never found out. But then came Grayson. How in God's name did he get it out of her? Pillow talk, he reckoned. Holland cursed the day that he'd invited Grayson to dinner and Felicity happened to drop by. Of course, he had to ask her to stick around. She and Grayson somehow hit it off that evening. It was exceedingly awkward to have his daughter dating his best friend, but what could he do? They were both adults, after all. But what did she see in him? He was thirty years older! Holland tried not to contemplate the obvious—that she was looking for a father figure. What did that say about him?

Well, at least the tabloids wouldn't report the romance. The guy that ran the *Star Globe* sold out for cheap. Holland offered him fifty thousand pounds and he took it, even though Holland had been prepared to go as high as one hundred thousand. But Holland knew it was only a matter of time. There were other tabloids. He couldn't buy them all off.

Anyway, Grayson knew who Holland really was and, in the face of his mounting debts, he'd threatened to let the secret out. Some best friend. Holland had been willing to kiss the six hundred thousand pounds goodbye. He'd only started writing the promissory notes because Grayson had insisted. "I want to make right my debts," Grayson had said at the beginning, like a good friend and a good man. Those were the days. They now seemed like a very long time ago. Since then, the addiction only got worse.

At first, Holland only knew about their card game debts. But then Grayson approached him one night at White's. "I know who your family is," he said. "Felicity told me. And you have to help me." And then he told Holland about the other debts. The three *million* pounds he'd lost gambling on everything under the sun. Horses, numbers, sporting events, everything. And who was the bookmaker? Who else? They practically owned the gaming industry in London and most of the UK. The Turner crime family. "You have to talk to them for me," Grayson had said that night at White's. He was scared. He was pale and shaky. "They're threatening me, John. They want their money. And I can't pay. I can't!" Then he'd started to cry. Holland had tried to explain that he never communicated with the Turners, but Grayson was desperate. In a fit of rage, he screamed, "If you don't talk to them, I'll tell everyone who you really are!"

Of course, that was more or less the end of their friendship. Holland had no choice but to contact his brother. Lennox Turner was the head honcho now. Their father had stepped aside, though he'd remained in a sort of advisory role. John and Lennox hadn't spoken for years, and the phone call was strained, to say the least. And not terribly long. "No dice, brother," Lennox had said before hanging up. Holland reported back to Grayson the next night at White's and that's when Grayson had proposed his preposterous idea. "Can't you just *ask* your mother for the money?" Holland had said. Well, apparently this wasn't the first time Grayson had been upside down with creditors. Buckingham Palace had bailed him out before, and the last time they'd done so, the queen had made it very clear that they would never do so again. Grayson was stuck.

Of course, Holland could square the debt himself, but that meant paying money out of his own funds to the family from whom he had sworn to remain apart. Damned if he was going to do that. Plus, how to explain the withdrawal? In the end, he decided to go along with the plan but insisted on informing his brother of what was happening. If they weren't going to forgive or restructure Grayson's debts, could they at least help in some way with his scheme? Wouldn't they want to protect their investment? And that's when Lennox had sent Andrew Quincy to oversee the project. "He's a good man," Lennox had said. "Just do what he says." Quincy seemed like a thug, but what could Holland do?

It was Quincy who suggested that the ransom note come from a third party, someone in no way connected with Grayson or Holland or the Turner family. Someone they could ultimately pin the kidnapping on if it all went south. Holland had to admit that it wasn't a bad idea. But who? And that's when he remembered the pledge he'd made to himself to exact his revenge on one Newton Dempsey. What an opportunity! Nobody makes John Holland look stupid and gets away with it. He had contacts in the States and it had come to his attention that Dempsey had recently been released from prison. Perfect timing. So Quincy sent Spenser Burke, a mobster wannabe, to Boston to get Dempsey. Burke's downfall was that he was not an officially sanctioned member of the Turner mob, and thus expendable. Once his job was done, well, so was he.

Lennox had determined that if they were going to do it, they needed to do it right. It was a prince, for God's sake, with access to the royal fortune. Lennox decided that the going rate for a prince was one hundred million dollars. It had to be dollars because that's what Dempsey would naturally ask for. But the amount was beyond audacious. It was absurd. Nobody agreed with Lennox Turner on the amount, but nobody disagreed either. You don't disagree with the head of the mob. You tell him, "Good idea," even if you think the idea is insane, which this plan most certainly was.

The kidnapping part had gone off without a hitch. Quincy was a bona fide sociopath, but he was clearly competent. Still, it was unnerving having to meet with him for updates. And he always insisted on meeting in the worst parts of town, like that hideous dive by the river in Rothton. Holland felt as if he needed a shower after those meetings.

Actually, there was one little hitch in the kidnapping. The fact that Buckingham Palace was not going to pay! Nobody had anticipated that. But here it was, approaching the 3 a.m. deadline that Lennox had now insisted upon and there was no sign of the money. Buckingham Palace hadn't even tried to negotiate.

Holland glanced over at Quincy holding that damn gun and felt a chill run up his spine. His instincts had always been accurate and, try as he might, he couldn't ignore those instincts now: this was not going to end well.

# 25

Prince Grayson, Earl of Kendal, fifth-born child of the queen of England, looked around the room in fear. Every man in this room loathed him, he could feel it. What was going to happen next? Why in the hell had Lennox Turner made Dempsey give Buckingham Palace that stupid 3 a.m. deadline? It was now 2:45. Why did he have to be so specific? The deadline was supposed to be today. That could mean *anytime* today. It could mean midnight twenty-one hours and fifteen minutes from now. Why not give them extra time? Why the sudden rush? Mum would take it as a slap in the face.

Certainly, the Lord Chamberlain of the Royal Household was busy getting the money together. Mum would insist on that, wouldn't she? Oh God, she had to. But what if they couldn't make Dempsey's new deadline? Getting a hundred million dollars together takes time, even if you're the queen of England. But of course, they'd been working on it all along undoubtedly. Sure, of course, they had.

Grayson wondered what he'd gotten himself into. The whole thing had taken on a life of its own. How did it all go so bad so quickly? A few unsuccessful bets here and there, mostly made in fun. But before he knew it, he was fifty thousand pounds in debt. Fifty thousand became a hundred thousand, which became half a million seemingly overnight. When Lennox Turner himself had threatened Grayson and told him the total was now three million, it shook him to his core. And now he was cut off. Turner would no longer allow him to place any bets. So how was he supposed to win his money back? How could he ever pay? "You know where to get the money," Turner had said, referencing the royal family. But of course, Turner didn't know that Mum had cut him off, too.

The only saving grace in the whole sordid business was Felicity. Sweet, beautiful Felicity. A ray of sunshine in his otherwise gloomy life. And when she told him who her father really was—his best friend, a member of the same family to whom he owed all his money? That was fate. That was meant to be. It was his reprieve from the gallows. Metaphorically speaking. He knew the actual means of his death would be more gruesome than hanging at the hands of the Turner family. All John had to do was make a phone call and take the heat off. A simple call. Brother to brother. But he couldn't do it. He couldn't make it happen.

Then Lennox had sent that goon Quincy around. A death threat would be one thing, but Quincy made it clear that the death would be preceded by hours of pain. And that's when the kidnapping plot sort of popped into his head. He didn't want to have to threaten John to go public with the revelation that he was really a Turner, but what choice did he have once John refused to help? Sure, John's reputation was on the line, but Prince Grayson's very *life* was on the line. Fortunately, John saw reason.

But then John got his brother involved in the plot and everything blew up. One hundred million dollars?! Grayson was in too deep to argue. He'd lost control of the plan. It was now Lennox's plan and he had to go along with it. Lennox sent Quincy by again to set everything up. It was agreed that Quincy would escort Grayson out of the manor house late one night using the secret passageway. They'd make it look like Grayson was taken out of the window. And then they'd hole up right here in Felicity's house while she went off to Norwich to stay with an old college roommate. He'd get his picture taken with Dempsey who would send the ransom note.

Of course, Quincy insisted that they make the kidnapping look especially real and when he came by that night, he hit Grayson on the forehead with the butt of his gun and then punched him in the nose, breaking it, producing blood and making it look like a struggle had occurred. Grayson sure hadn't expected that. Holding his nose and trying to stem the bleeding from his forehead, he'd said, "Was that really necessary?" Quincy, that psycho, had shrugged and grinned. "Maybe, maybe not."

And now it was 2:50. Nobody was saying a word. Each man sensed the tension in the room. When Quincy's phone rang, everybody jumped but Quincy who calmly answered.

"Yes?" *Finally*, Quincy thought. This was the call he had been expecting. Lennox was going to give him his orders. And, frankly, he wasn't surprised by them. Not in the least. He looked around the room at the three nervous men while listening to his boss.

"I have 2:52," Lennox was saying. "I'd be shocked if the old woman came through in the next eight minutes. If the money's not in the account now, it's never going to be. Even so, have Dempsey send one more threat exactly at three. Give them two additional minutes. No more. Understood?"

"Yes, sir."

"And after those two minutes, we're finished. Right? I mean *finished.*"

"Even . . . you know?"

"John stopped being my brother years ago."

"Understood."

"Then clean it all up. I'll send a couple guys to help. Then get the hell out of there. Call me when it's done."

"Yes, boss."

The two hung up and Dempsey tentatively asked, "What did Lennox have to say?"

"Oh, nothing, really," Quincy replied. "He was just asking for an update. And he wants you to send one more email at three o'clock on the nose, giving them two extra minutes."

Grayson groaned. What the hell difference was that going to make? Mum wasn't going to pay and that was that. She'd made it clear her whole life that England does not negotiate with terrorists. And she meant it, even if it meant the end of her son. And this certainly was the end. Grayson looked over at Quincy, still holding the gun on his lap.

Then he happened to glance over at Dempsey whose eyes were focused on his laptop. A strange expression was coming over his face.

Was that . . . a smile?

"God almighty," Dempsey said, his eyes getting wide.

Everyone sat up. "What?" said Holland.

"It's there!" Dempsey replied, his face breaking into a wide grin. "Well, half of it is anyway. It's in the account! Fifty million! There's an email. They say they'll give the balance when the prince is delivered safe and sound."

"Bullshit," said Quincy. "They won't pay the balance."

"Who cares?" said Grayson. "Didn't you hear the man?! It's fifty bloody million!"

Holland and Grayson both came out of their chairs and stood behind Dempsey, gazing over his shoulder at his laptop, needing to see their miraculous deliverance with their own eyes.

Grayson started to tear up. "I knew she'd pay," he sniffed. "I just knew she would."

Quincy pulled out his phone and called his boss who agreed with Quincy that they wouldn't get the balance, but fifty million was fifty million so why rock the boat? "Sneak Grayson out of there and drop him off at the manor," Lennox ordered. "Tell him we never want to see him again. Tell my brother that a deal is a deal and that I'll be wiring a sum of money into his account within twenty-four hours. After that, I never want to see or hear from him, either. Whatever he wants to do with Dempsey is up to him. Maybe you can offer your services."

"Right, boss," Quincy said and hung up. Grayson had grabbed a bottle of champagne off the shelf and was uncorking it. "I knew it!" he exclaimed. "I knew all along it would work! I knew Mum would pay." He took a swig out of the bottle and handed it to Holland. "John, I hope all is forgiven, old sport. Things were desperate, you know. I had no choice. They were going to kill me. But it all worked out, didn't it? My idea worked! Everybody wins." He was beaming.

Holland took the bottle. "I suppose so," he said, taking a swallow. "But this is one sordid affair I'm very happy to put behind me."

Dempsey grabbed the bottle from Holland and took a swig himself. "And this squares us, right, Holland?"

"Get something straight, Dempsey," Holland snapped. "I don't like you. You're a piece of bloody shite as far as I'm concerned. A thief and a cheat."

"Okay, sure, but we had a deal, John. Safe passage out of the country and on to Costa Rica, remember? That was the agreement. And I did my part."

"Of course. Safe passage to Costa Rica." Holland shot a glance at Quincy. He'd made a deal, all right. He'd made a deal with Quincy who, as it happened, had already offered his services to Holland ahead of Lennox's suggestion.

"Put down the bottle, gents," Quincy said, getting out of his chair. "We have to get the prince back to the manor. Prince, you'll tell everyone that Dempsey here let you go and that he acted alone."

"Of course."

Then he waved toward Holland and Dempsey. "Then you two will go back with me to Holland's place."

"And work on getting me out of the country," said Dempsey. "Right?"

"Sure," Quincy said. "Sure. Now let's get going."

"Need a lift?"

The four men spun toward the front of the room to see Kori Briggs and Anya Kovalev, Anya with her gun pointed directly at Quincy.

"Of course, we'll be taking a little detour to the police station first," Kori continued, striding over to Quincy and taking back her Glock. "I hope you took good care of him," she said. "He's my best friend, you know."

In an instant, the room became a cacophony of boisterous discord.

"Thank God you're here!" Dempsey roared. "These guys put me up to this and I'm pretty damn sure that John Holland here was going to have me killed!"

Holland pointed to Quincy. "This man is responsible! I'm the victim of extortion!"

"Please take me home!" Grayson pleaded. "This has all been a perfectly frightful experience! I really need to just lie down."

Quincy stood silent, moving ever so slightly toward the far end of the room. The other three continued to shout above each other, pointing fingers and professing innocence. Finally, Kori put her thumb and forefinger in her mouth and blew a piercing whistle. "Save it," she said. "You're all going down to Thames House."

"Oh, but surely not me," said Grayson.

"Especially you, Prince. We've been out in the entryway for a while. We heard it all. Ah, and here's your ride now." Two uniformed police officers entered the room.

Everyone turned toward them and the shouting began anew.

"But I'm an innocent victim!" pleaded the prince.

"Extortion!" proclaimed Holland.

"You should talk!" screamed Dempsey. "If there was anyone extorted, it was me! In fact, *I'm* the kidnapping victim here!"

"You're a worthless liar!" Holland fired back. "You've always been a worthless liar!"

"An innocent victim!" the prince pleaded again. "Surely that is obvious!"

"I can't listen to any more of this," said Kori. "Get 'em outa here, boys. All four of them."

"Begging your pardon, miss," one of the officers said, "Four, did you say?"

Kori and Anya whirled around. Quincy was gone.

"Crap!" Kori said. Turning to Holland, she pointed to the door at the rear of the room. "Where's that lead?"

"Back stairwell. Goes to the alley in the rear of the house."

"Come on, Anya!"

The two dashed out of the back of the room and flew down the stairs. They barreled through the back door and out into the alley. Anya looked left and spied a shadow running away from them.

"There!" she said. Both agents began to run down the alley. Anya fired a warning shot. "Halt!" she shouted, but the figure turned at the end of the block and began sprinting down the main street.

Anya and Kori followed with Anya running about ten feet ahead of Kori. In the low lighting from the streetlamps, they could see the silhouetted figure of Andrew Quincy running across the street. He dove behind a parked car, then raised up and Kori could make out something in his hand.

"He's got a gun!" she shouted to Anya, suddenly wishing they had frisked Quincy when they had the chance. Of course, he would have another gun.

Anya brought her weapon up but as she did so, Kori saw a flash from behind the parked car across the street. Anya grunted and fell to the ground.

"Anya!" Kori cried out.

The figure rose from behind the car and began running again. Kori crossed the street, rage coursing through her body. She drew her Glock, and as the figure neared the ring of light from the next streetlamp, she raised it and aimed. "You son of a *bitch!*" she snarled. Then she pulled the trigger and watched as the figure of Andrew Quincy crumpled to the pavement.

# 26

— · —

"The queen will see you now," the private secretary to the queen, a tall, immaculately dressed man with a receding hairline, said coming out from the royal stateroom at the palace.

"Okay," Kori said, straightening her dress, something she didn't wear very often. The waiting room was bigger than her DC apartment, with thick, plush, red carpeting, high ceilings with gold leaf gilding, and mirrored walls.

"Now, do you remember the etiquette we went over?" asked the private secretary. "Do not offer your hand unless the queen offers hers first. A curtsey is always appreciated. You will refer to her initially as 'Your Royal Highness.' From that point on, you are to call her 'Ma'am.' Allow her to lead the conversation. She will express her appreciation for all that you've done and then, as we discussed, present you with the Most Excellent Order of the British Empire for Chivalry and Gallantry. I imagine she'll engage with you in some small talk. Make your answers brief. Do not ask personal questions. When she is finished, you will know. You'll give a slight bow, perhaps another curtsey, and then walk toward the door you entered, careful not to turn your back on the queen as you are leaving. Any questions?"

"Nope," Kori said, taking a deep breath. "Sounds pretty straightforward to me." Then she glanced beside her. "Well? You heard the man. Any questions?"

"Just one," Anya Kovalev replied. "The curtsey . . . it might be a little difficult with these crutches, no?"

"A nod of the head will do just fine," the private secretary smiled. "The queen completely understands. Now, if you'll please both follow me."

Anya's upper thigh wound would heal nicely, though she wouldn't be engaging in any serious physical activity for a while.

Andrew Quincy would spend three weeks in Wellington Hospital. Kori's bullet, aimed at the heart, tore through a rib and punctured a lung. After release from Wellington, he would spend several more weeks recovering in the Belmarsh Prison hospital, which was convenient because Belmarsh Prison is where he would be sentenced to serve a life term for the kidnapping of Prince Grayson and the murder of Agent Victor Graham of MI5. He refused a lighter prison sentence in exchange for testifying against Lennox Turner believing—correctly, no doubt—that testifying against Lennox Turner would have been tantamount to a death sentence. Instead, he pleaded guilty to both counts.

Meanwhile, Lennox Turner's fingerprints were nowhere on the kidnapping and the Turner crime family would continue business as usual. Wealthier, in fact, to the tune of fifty million dollars since nobody would ever trace the overseas account to them. But they'd never get the second fifty million. Turner had been right that the queen had no intention of paying the balance. Hudson Imports was summarily shut down, but would reappear later as Grayson Imports, partly in honor of the man responsible for the sudden infusion of cash to the Turner organization, but mostly in jest and mockery.

Delivering Newton Dempsey to the queen all wrapped up with a red, white, and blue bow, as Kori had promised the president, wasn't exactly practical or appropriate. Nonetheless, the queen told both Kori and Anya she was "exceedingly grateful" for the resolution of the case as they received their Most Excellent Orders of the British Empire. The queen, as it happened, was well aware of Rampart and the work they did. She had known about the agency since its inception under the Kennedy administration. She regretted not being able to publicly acknowledge the role that Kori and Anya had played, but she understood and respected the secretive nature of their organization.

Dempsey would be remanded to the custody of MI5. Kori would speak to Director Eaglethorpe about Dempsey's forced participation in the scheme. Dempsey, it seemed to Kori, was actually the real kidnapping victim, just as he'd said he was. And certainly destined for a mob-style execution had the agents not come along when they did. Eaglethorpe would speak to the president who would speak to the PM. In exchange for testifying privately against Andrew Quincy, Dempsey would be turned over to the US under one condition: he was never to talk publicly about the events of the kidnapping plot. Then he was sent home where he reclaimed his job at the South Boston car dealership. He had dinner occasionally with his brother, Russell, and sister-in-law, Helen, the latter forever maintaining a healthy mistrust.

For weeks, Dempsey had to explain to anyone who asked, often complete strangers, why his picture had been splashed all over as a person of interest in the kidnapping of England's Prince Grayson. "Well, you see, I went to London on vacation," went his story, "and happened to meet this guy Quincy at a pub one night. Quite accidentally. Just got to talking, you know. Well, I guess the police were following him around that night so they took a picture of me figuring we were best friends or something. Wrong place, wrong time. Just a big misunderstanding, really. Afterward, the cops realized I couldn't possibly have had anything to do with the kidnapping and they apologized profusely." It was lame by Dempsey's standards, but he was done concocting fanciful stories. Besides, it took only about a month before people stopped asking and the public's attention focused on the next big story the media were pushing.

Sir John Holland had too much information on the prince for Buckingham Palace to risk a public trial and too much money to be prosecuted. Everyone knew that Holland could put together a team of the best barristers in all of England. And so in the end, his name was kept completely out of the record. And that meant the name "Turner" never came up, either. The palace made good on the promissory notes with the understanding that Holland, too, would never speak publicly about the events. It was never known whether his brother, Lennox, shared any of the ransom money with him as he had said he would. When you're a billionaire, the addition of a few more million doesn't make a visible difference in your lifestyle, especially when you're something of a recluse, which Holland became even more of as the months and years went on.

Prince Grayson, Earl of Kendal, was remanded to the custody of his mother. She secretly had him whisked away to a residential treatment program for his gambling addiction, followed by outpatient care, followed by weekly counseling sessions, and intensive cognitive behavioral therapy. He sought counseling as well for the deep depression that had fallen upon him as a result of the plot gone bad coupled with the heartbreak of losing the love of his life. Felicity Watts, after a rather generous payday from Buckingham Palace to maintain her silence, moved permanently to Norwich and never had anything to do with Prince Grayson again.

As far as the public knew, a lone actor by the name of Andrew Quincy, a two-bit hustler from Southwark, carried off the kidnapping. The "person of interest" whose face had been presented by the police was presumed to be a friend of his but was, in the end, exonerated. Following up on leads they'd uncovered in their relentless investigating, MI5 had found and rescued the prince from a private home in St. John's Wood where a subsequent shootout with Quincy landed him in the hospital. The officers who had effected the rescue were decorated by the queen, as was the original head of the MI5 kidnapping task force, Victor Graham, posthumously.

Security measures were beefed up around Prince Grayson's manor. A new alarm system and security cameras were installed. The prince was in no position to object. As for his staff, Parker Bates resumed his duties as private secretary, remaining as loyal as always. Kingsley Moore moved back into the manor, happy to be out of his sister's house and away from the ever-present, headache-inducing banging of the piano. And Charles and Violet Stewart took up residency again, comfortable once more in their quarters, even more so now with their brand-new, fifty-five-inch flat-screen TV.

Kori stuck around for a few days after the arrest of Quincy, one, to see to it that Anya was healing up; two, to receive her Most Excellent Order commendation; and, three, to spend what turned out to be a very romantic evening with her favorite London bobby, Sargent Fletcher

Willis. She couldn't tell him very much about the case, but Fletch, as she repeatedly called him, more or less figured it all out anyway.

Fletch took her to the Hide Restaurant in Mayfair and the two talked easily, their conversation ranging from history and philosophy to art and music. At one point, Fletch talked about his life as a bobby. His father had been one and his grandfather before him. Law enforcement was a proud family tradition. Fletch was applying to be a detective, a member of the criminal investigation department. The family had money from his mother's side and he'd traveled extensively throughout Europe as a child. But he loved London most of all. "She's a grand lady," he said.

Kori picked up the check in appreciation of Fletch possibly saving her life in the alley that day. After dinner, she took him back to her hotel and showed her appreciation again, and in no uncertain terms. The next morning, they promised each other they'd keep in touch. "And I'll come back to London soon," Kori offered. She meant it sincerely, even though she knew deep down that the odds of a return trip any time soon were long; there was no telling where duty would take her next. Nevertheless, it was nice knowing Fletch would be there. It was nice knowing there was a man in London.

Two days after Kori returned to the States, she met with her mother for dinner at Martin's Tavern in Georgetown. Over the restaurant's slow-roasted pot roast and a bottle of cabernet sauvignon, the two chatted and caught up. Kori presented a fictionalized account of her time in Boston representing the Gladstone Conveyor Company and Joan talked about her gardening, rambling on for a while about her peonies. Then she changed gears and talked about her book club.

"We're reading a spy thriller," Joan remarked. "It's good. Interestingly, the main character is a female agent."

"Oh, yeah?"

"Yep. I like her, but I think she swears too much. It's the F-word every other sentence."

"Well, I guess some people like it that way," Kori said. "You know, supposedly makes it more gritty, more urban."

"If I wanted gritty and urban I'd hang out at the bus depot."

"I hear ya, Mom."

"But, listen, Kori, did you hear the latest on the prince?"

"The prince? Only something about how he was kidnapped but that they rescued him and caught the kidnapper. The prince is back home safe and sound, right?"

"Right. But, Kori, there's much more to the story."

"Oh?"

"Much more. They caught the kidnapper, all right. Apparently, he'd been keeping the prince in a home not far from the prince's mansion. Anyway, the cops burst in and the kidnapper tried to flee and they gunned him down in the street outside."

"Wow."

"Yes, except it wasn't the police that gunned him down, Kori."

"No?"

"No. Get a load of this. The *Star Globe* reported that two mysterious women chased him. Women in civilian clothes, neither of whom had been seen before or since."

*Son-of-a-bitch Riley followed us!* Kori thought.

"And it was one of the women who shot him," Joan continued. "A reporter from the *Star Globe* just happened to be passing by at the time. Unfortunately, he didn't have his camera with him, so there are no pictures."

Kori stifled a chuckle. "Well, Mom, that's really something. So who do you think the women were?"

"Well they couldn't have been with the police or their presence would have been in the news."

"True."

"So they must have been with some other organization. But since nobody besides the *Star Globe* is talking about them, it must be a secret agency. The *Star Globe* said as much. A secret spy agency, Kori. Can you imagine?"

Kori laughed. "Mom, you know what? I think you're reading too many spy novels."

"Maybe . . ."

"Listen, let's grab the waiter and check out the dessert menu, what do you say? Maybe they still have that bread pudding you like. And, Mom, I'm dying to hear more about those peonies of yours."

"Really?"

"Yes! Tell me what your secret is. And don't spare any details. I want to hear all about them!"

"Sure. Well, of course, it starts with the right soil . . ."

Kori smiled, picked up the bottle of cabernet, and poured them each another glass. Then she leaned back in her chair, happy to be hearing about peonies or, well, anything besides spies and secret agencies and gossip reporters and kidnapped princes.

**The Kori Briggs series of adventure spy novels
by A.P. Rawls:**

### *The Dark Tetrad*

In this action-packed Kori Briggs debut novel, Kori is on the trail of a madman who has managed to steal a hundred pounds of uranium and, with the help of an equally twisted Russian scientist, is intent on detonating a nuclear bomb somewhere in the world. But when and where? Come along with Kori on this vicarious thrill ride as she follows clues from Washington, DC to New York City, Russia, Israel, and finally, Paris, the "City of Lights."

### *We'll Quit When We're Dead*

Everyone's favorite secret agent is once again globetrotting around the world to save the day. This time she's investigating a real and imminent threat from a foreign power, a potential terrorist act on American soil so extensive that its successful deployment could well result in World War III. Follow Kori from San Francisco to Vancouver to Istanbul as she races against time to prevent a cataclysmic collision with destiny.

*Danger Level 4*

In this third book of the A.P. Rawls series of Kori Briggs suspense spy thrillers, Kori has landed in the middle of a South American revolution. Super-secret spy organization Rampart has intelligence that a dictator with weapons of mass destruction is about to be overthrown. But who are the revolutionaries, and are they any less dangerous? The stability of the Western Hemisphere is at stake. Follow Kori through the jungles, hills, and perilous streets of a nation on the brink of war with itself!

*The Prince is Missing!*

In this fourth book of the series, Kori has been tasked with the assignment of finding England's missing Prince Grayson! All signs point to a kidnapping at the hands of an American ex-con, but Kori knows there's much more to the story. Follow her and her trusty Russian sidekick Anya Kovalev as they scour the grand city of London for clues to the prince's disappearance!

**Get a free gift when you register for updates at https://koribriggs.com/connect/**

**UWS**
**Upper West Side Press, LLC**

www.ingramcontent.com/pod-product-compliance
Lightning Source LLC
Chambersburg PA
CBHW051140190726
48290CB00006B/1927